Praise for *Hollyland*

"*Hollyland* is a treasure. I stayed up all night to finish it down. What I thought would be a chick-lit romp turned out to be a delightful, romantic, inspiring story I can't stop thinking about. This book is a love letter to art, creativity, and passion. The characters come alive on the page and leave you wanting more. Leavy is a genius."

—Jessica Smartt Gullion, author of *October Birds*

"Leavy has penned a whimsical and engaging adult fairy tale that explores the search for magic or gold dust in our lives. *Hollyland* is an endlessly entertaining romp down the yellow brick road as the characters search for passion in all forms. Romance meets comedy meets suspense, with oodles of inspiration thrown in for good measure. This book was so captivating that I read it in one sitting, and the ending was so satisfying, I wanted to read it again."

—U. Melissa Anyiwo, editor of *Gender Warriors*

"Author Patricia Leavy does an excellent job of building up her characters in this enthralling romance novel . . . the story is alluring and enchanting. . . . *Hollyland* takes the opposites attract trope to a new level by creating characters that are deep and compelling against an intriguing Hollywood backdrop. This will make a perfect feel-good beach read. . . . *Hollyland* is a novel that left me smiling."

—Literary Titan, 4-star review

"Some fun secondary characters, a well-drawn setting, and an exciting eleventh-hour kidnapping plot propel Leavy's story. The author also offers rich details about Rye's Hollywood world and Dee's opinions on art . . ."

—*Kirkus Reviews*

"*Hollyland* is a rip-roaring ride through hilarious, romantic, and sometimes downright mysterious ups and downs. With the right amount of awe, giggles, and laugh-out-loud moments, *Hollyland* shines. Whether you come for the comedy or the sexy and sweet romance, Dee and those she holds dear will wrap you up in a hug and tug on your emotions from cover to cover."

—J. E. Sumerau, author of *Scarecrow*

"*Hollyland* is one of the best love stories I've read. I could not put this book down. Leavy has crafted a riveting story about never settling in love or art. A light and surprisingly provocative book for smart and sassy readers. Absolutely brilliant."

—Sandra L. Faulkner, author of *Real Women Run*

"Leavy is a master at penning love stories that are so much more. She writes light, hope, and optimism in every corner. *Hollyland* is the novel we've been hoping Leavy, an acclaimed arts researcher, would write. It's a beautiful romance appropriate for anyone looking for joy, escape, and inspiration. It's also an important statement about the role of the arts in our lives. Every art educator and artist should read this book. Highly recommended!"

—Jessie Voigts, PhD, founder of Wandering Educators

HOLLYLAND

HOLLYLAND

A Novel

Patricia Leavy

SHE WRITES PRESS

Published 2023
Printed in the United States of America
Print ISBN: 978-1-64742-296-7
E-ISBN: 978-1-64742-297-4
Library of Congress Control Number: 2022913706

For information, address:
She Writes Press
1569 Solano Ave #546
Berkeley, CA 94707

Interior Design by Kiran Spees

She Writes Press is a division of SparkPoint Studio, LLC.

For my father,
Bob Leavy,
always an optimist

Part One

1

DEE CLUTCHED HER CELL PHONE AND EXITED THE crowded bar to see a line of hopefuls waiting to get in. Looking for a quiet place to take her call, she walked around the corner to the empty side street, the warm LA breeze blowing through her long, chestnut hair. Just as she put the phone to her ear, actor Ryder Field stepped out of the side entrance. With a string of film credits to his name, he was best known for the twelve years he starred as CIA operative Bruce Jones on the hit action television series *The Mission.* Examining his tight black jeans and black T-shirt that showed off his muscular, tattooed arms, Dee couldn't help but notice how impossibly sexy he was. They made eye contact, and she looked down ever so slightly. He smiled at her, and then leaned against the stucco exterior of the building and lit a cigarette.

"Uh, hi. I'm here," she said, trying to refocus on her call. "Are they freaking out? . . . I guess you haven't read it yet," she said with a chuckle. "Well, yeah, you could say that. It might be a *little* provocative. As soon as we hang up, I'll text you the bits you should be aware of . . . Right now? . . . Jesus, just let me text you in a minute . . . Fine." She glanced over at Ryder, who smiled and took a drag of his cigarette. She looked away, lowered her voice, and said, "On page one, there's an explicit oral act in the balcony of a church. Page four, bent over a pew . . . No, the other thing. Page seven, on the altar . . ." She glanced up at Ryder, who was staring at her and trying to keep a straight face, laughter in his sea-colored eyes. "Well, tell them it's not technically forbidden in the Bible. I don't think it's expressly mentioned . . . Oh, one more thing. Holy water is used as a metaphor throughout . . . Think about it . . . Yeah." She laughed nervously. "Oh, I can imagine the subject line of that email! . . . Well, just tell them, 'Toto, we're not in Kansas anymore.'" She laughed again. "Yeah, okay. Thanks, bye," she finished, hanging up.

She looked sheepishly at Ryder. He turned to face her and leaned his shoulder against the building. "Sorry about that," she said.

"I have a million questions about that call," he said.

She smiled. "Have a good night," she said as she turned to leave.

"Wait! You can't leave me wondering like that. You're not going to tell me?"

She swiveled to face him. "Not much to tell. The editorial board at my publishing house in New York is a little concerned about some of the content in my latest book. Same story, new day."

"Sounds like a hell of a book."

She giggled. "Honestly, it's not as salacious at it sounds. If they didn't get distracted so easily, they'd see it's really just a sweet little story about identity in America."

"Then why, uh, push the envelope?"

She shrugged. "Because I can. I don't need another reason."

He smiled and looked down, his face turning red.

"I love art more than anything; it's sacred to me. Artists need to be free. Art shouldn't have to apologize for itself. It should provoke, inspire, unsettle, and disrupt—or at least aspire to," she explained.

"What about entertain?"

"Sure, that too. Of course, art and entertainment aren't always the same thing, are they?"

He looked at her intently as if she had just asked a question that he had been asking himself for years.

She continued, "I just mean that as soon as you're thinking about entertaining, you're thinking about audience. Sometimes art gets watered down to appeal to the masses or to placate the people holding the purse strings. It's hard to be truthful or to follow your own creative heart if you're too concerned by what others might think. Let's just say that I've never been terribly interested in what's trendy. There's no place for that when making art."

"I'm Ryder Field. My friends call me Rye," he said, dropping his cigarette butt, stepping forward, and extending his hand.

"I've seen some of your work. Dee Schwartz," she said, shaking his hand.

"So, you're a writer?"

"Actually, I'm an arts researcher. I've written and lectured about the relationship between art and science, but I also dabble in poetry and fiction."

"Did you study art in school?" he asked.

"I guess I'm a bit of a mutt. In college, I majored in psychology with minors in neuroscience and creative writing, and then I got my doctorate in art education."

"Wow, that's quite a résumé," he said, his eyes wide. "Not the typical LA story. I'm impressed."

"Don't be. It was just a convoluted way to help people understand art so they could better appreciate it, especially in education. In truth, I was chasing something deceptively simple yet elusive, maybe something you can never hold on to."

"What's that?" he asked, hanging on her every word.

"Magic." He looked at her like she'd just said something he'd never be able to forget. "That probably sounds silly," she said, biting her lip.

"Not in the slightest," he replied. "I've been doing that my whole life, chasing that same kind of magic."

"Is that why you became an actor?"

"Like you, I love art. I especially love storytelling. Couldn't picture myself doing anything else." He looked down, huffed, and said, "Honestly, I was probably a little terrified of anything ordinary. I suppose I wanted to live an extraordinary life."

"That's kind of funny, don't you think?"

He furrowed his brow.

"That you wanted to live an extraordinary life, as opposed to wanting to be an extraordinary person."

"Huh. I don't know what to say to that," he admitted bashfully.

"I'm sorry. That probably came out wrong."

"On the contrary," he said. He looked at her intently. "I feel a bit tongue-tied around you. I've only known you for a few minutes, but I don't think I'll ever be able to forget this conversation, starting with that book of yours, which I've got to read."

She laughed. They stared at each other for a long moment, palpable, electric energy between them. The breeze blew her hair across her face, and he reached out and gently tucked it behind her ear. "Uh, the band's probably coming on soon. I should go back in," she said quietly.

"Wait." He grabbed her hand, his body practically touching hers. He caressed her cheek, leaned forward, and lightly pressed his mouth to hers. "I probably should have asked you before I did that," he said.

"Do it again."

He cupped her face in his hands and kissed her softly. "I'm friends with the band. Come backstage and watch the show with me."

"My friends are waiting for me inside," she said.

"Bring them with you. My friends would love to meet you."

"I'm a little shy, actually."

"All evidence to the contrary," he said, flashing a million-dollar smile. "You know what? I have a better idea. Let's go somewhere more private. Go tell your friends you're leaving, and then meet me back here."

"What about the band?"

"They'll understand." He ran his finger along her cheek and said, "I know it's crazy, but you feel it too, right?"

"Feel what?" she asked.

"Magic."

She smiled and said, "Give me ten minutes."

"Thank God you're back, Dee. Sara's been boring me to tears, complaining about her students. Please save me before my ears bleed," Troy said, taking a swig of his cocktail.

Sara rolled her eyes. "We were starting to wonder if you bailed on us."

"Funny you should say that," Dee said, plopping into her seat. "Actually, I met someone. He wants me to meet him outside in ten minutes so we can go somewhere quieter."

"Text me a picture of his license plate. Keep an eye on your drink. Use a condom," Troy instructed matter-of-factly.

Sara shot him a disapproving look. "Dee, you can't be serious. You're going to leave with some random guy you just met? He could be psychotic."

"Well, I guess he's not *totally* random," she said sheepishly. "It's Ryder Field, the actor."

"In that case, don't use a condom. Have lots and lots of babies with him," Troy said.

Sara punched his arm.

"What? He's Hollywood royalty! You know who his family is, and he's sexy as all hell. I've fantasized about him for years," Troy said.

"Sorry, I don't think he's gay," Dee replied.

"He is in my fantasies," Troy quipped, sipping his drink.

"Have you two lost your minds?" Sara asked. "Dee, allow me to inject a little reality into this situation. He's obviously a player. What good could come from this? Let me remind you, he dumped his wife for America's sweetheart herself, Krysta Dunn. Then, when she broke off their engagement, he got married to that porn star in Vegas, Bailey something, Britney something, what was her name?"

"Bentley Barnes," Troy said, "but he got that annulled. It was just a weekend gone awry. Who hasn't had one of those?"

Dee laughed.

Troy continued, "I'm impressed that you're up-to-date on your celeb gossip, Sara."

"Common knowledge. You can't help it when it's splashed on the cover of every magazine at the grocery store checkout," Sara said.

Dee stared her down. "Oh, please, you read all those trashy magazines whenever you go on vacation. You always bring great works of literature and then swap them out for *Celebs Weekly* and those other rags when you think no one's looking." Sara blushed and Dee continued, "Besides, those relationships were decades ago. He was in his twenties. He's gotta be approaching fifty by now."

"I'll tell you," Troy said, scrolling away on his phone. "Google is the gift that keeps on giving. Here we go. He married aspiring actress Sascha Winston, who no one's ever heard of, when he was twenty-one;

he left her when he was twenty-six after meeting Krysta Dunn on a film set. They were engaged for two years, during which time her star exploded into the stratosphere. She called off their wedding on the day of, practically leaving him at the altar. Six months later, he had his little drunken Vegas mishap, which he annulled after seventy-two hours. He was thirty when his run on *The Mission* began, and he became one of the biggest stars in the world and everyone's favorite hero, the invincible Bruce Jones. The rest is history."

"You know, I've seen a few of his movies, but I've never seen a single episode of *The Mission*," Dee said.

"Honey, you really need to put down the books and pick up the remote. All the man candy is on TV. When you get home, stream *The Mission*. Your boy is hot as hell, a modern-day superhero. Anyway," Troy continued, looking at his phone, "since his Vegas fiasco, he's had a string of model-slash-actress girlfriends, most recently thirty-four-year-old actress wannabe Lucy Vega, who is drop-dead beautiful. They lived together for four years."

"Did you really have to add the drop-dead beautiful part?" Dee asked.

"Sorry, love. If it helps, I snooped on Lucy's Instagram account. She only has three thousand followers, and most of them have names like RyderLove and BruceJonesForever. Ooh, and there are a bunch of interviews with him saying they never married because he doesn't ever want to get married again."

"What did I tell you? A player," Sara said with an air of vindication.

Dee rolled her eyes.

"And he just turned fifty; he's exactly ten years older than you," Troy said, sliding his phone back into his pocket.

"Why don't you tell her about his infamous fights with the paparazzi? Didn't that come up in your search? He's assaulted a bunch of people. He's known for being aggressive and hotheaded. This guy is a classic Hollywood bad boy. Dee, you're kind and reserved. It would never work."

"She's not always so reserved," Troy protested. He turned to Dee, smiled, and said, "My love, you're bold in your work."

"I wasn't reserved with him. We kissed. Twice," Dee said, blushing.

"I'll drink to that," Troy pronounced, raising his glass.

Sara shook her head in disbelief. "You're a scholar, for goodness' sake! What could you two possibly have in common?"

"I don't know, but I want to find out," Dee said wistfully. "There was something between us, something I haven't felt in a long time, if ever. Celebrity has never impressed me, it's not that. It's him."

"Go. Have fun. Take notes. Hell, take videos," Troy said, raising his glass and smiling.

Sara wore a defiant grimace on her face.

"Don't worry about us," Troy insisted. "A couple more drinks and I'll get her to turn that frown upside down."

Sara shook her head and laughed. "Just be safe."

Dee gave them both a quick hug and left. She burst out into the warm night air and walked around the corner. Rye was standing in front of the passenger door of a black Porsche. He smiled brightly, opened the door for her, and she got in.

2

"COME ON IN," RYE SAID, TOSSING THE TAKEOUT BAG on the entry table and turning off the alarm.

"Your house is beautiful," she said, looking around the spotless, contemporary Beverly Hills mansion that boasted high ceilings, wood floors, and expansive windows, everything neatly in its place, right down to the vase of perfectly arranged white flowers on the entry table.

"Thank you," he said. "I spend so much of my life on the road, on location. I've tried to create a peaceful sanctuary back home."

She noticed a few small framed photographs on the credenza and smiled. "This is a great piece," she said, admiring the large modern painting hanging in the foyer: a fuchsia strip and a few black squiggles across a white canvas.

He came up beside her and put his hand on her back as if it were completely natural. "Thank you. My taste is pretty minimalist."

"Mine too," she said.

"But I like surprises, a little something bold."

"Me too."

He kissed her cheek. They lingered for a moment, relishing the touch, and then he grabbed the takeout, took her hand, and said, "Let's go eat."

Rye turned the lights on dimly as they strolled into the massive kitchen, a chef's dream with sleek, modern appliances, a white tile backsplash, white cabinetry, and light gray walls. Dee ran her hand along the polished marble island. "Do you cook?"

"Afraid not, although I can make a pretty good breakfast," he said. "You?"

"Yeah, I love to cook."

"Come, sit," he said, guiding her to the table. He retrieved dishes and silverware and set them out. "I feel like the cheapest date ever," he remarked, unwrapping their burgers and placing the container of fries between them. "Takeout from a drive-through is pretty lame."

"Actually, I think it's perfect. It's nice to be somewhere quiet."

He leaned down and kissed her gently, as if he'd been doing it for years. "I can make up for it with a great bottle of wine. Red or white?"

"Red, please."

He grabbed two crystal goblets, scoured his wine cellar before selecting a Rioja, and then uncorked the bottle. "This is Spanish, medium-bodied. We should probably let it breathe for a minute. I hope you like it," he said as he placed the glasses on the table, poured the wine, and sat down.

"Are you a big wine drinker?" she asked.

"I'm more of a whiskey guy, but I can appreciate something special," he said, taking her hand. They stared into each other's eyes like they might never look away. He cleared his throat. "Uh, the wine is probably ready. How about a toast?"

She nodded.

"To something special," he said.

She smiled. "To something special."

They clinked glasses and took a sip. "Ooh, that's delicious," she said.

"Glad you like it. Shall we?" he asked, picking up his burger.

She cut hers in half, picked up a piece, and took a bite.

"I promise you a better meal next time," he said. "So, tell me about yourself."

"What do you want to know?" she asked, wiping her mouth.

"Everything."

She looked down, nervously biting her lip. "I'm usually pretty timid. This isn't like me at all."

"You didn't seem so shy on that phone call, or when you were schooling me about art."

She laughed. "I didn't mean to come off . . ."

"Don't apologize," he said, taking her hand. "It was enchanting."

"My work is the one place where I don't hold back. In the rest of my life . . ."

"What?" he asked, massaging her fingers.

"Let's just say that in a crowded room, you'd find me sitting quietly in the corner, perfectly content. Pretty different from you, I imagine. You have 'live out loud' written all over you. The spotlight suits you."

He blushed. "There you go again."

"What?"

"Making me feel tongue-tied. I've never been at a loss for words until you came along." They sat for a moment, looking at each other. He rubbed the palm of her hand before releasing it. "Sometimes I long for quiet moments. Most people know me as the loud guy at the table; I can't remember the last time I spent a day alone, but there's another side that people rarely see. Maybe it's why we met—for balance."

She beamed.

"Where are you from?" he asked.

"New York. Manhattan."

"Tell me about your family," he said, taking a bite of his burger.

"Well, I'm an only child. I'm really close to my dad. He's from

Brooklyn. His dad dropped out of school in the seventh grade after his father split. My grandfather took a menial job to take care of his mother and sisters, so my dad and his older brother didn't have much growing up. My uncle was a hustler, always looking for easy money, shortcuts, or so I've been told. Died young in a street fight. I never knew him, but I think his death motivated my dad, who believed there weren't shortcuts to anywhere worth going. Education was everything to him, a way to something better. He put himself through public college, and then earned an MBA. He loves literature and history, always has his nose in a book, but he wanted to captain his own ship, to control his own destiny, so he and one of his classmates started a small publishing company in Manhattan." She shook her head and chuckled. "They each invested five thousand dollars, which took my father eons to save. They built it into a major publishing house, bootstrapping the whole thing, never taking any venture capital. About five years ago, they sold it for over fifty million dollars."

"Wow, that's incredible."

"He's an amazing man. It's a lot to live up to."

"He must be proud of you."

"Yeah, I think he is," she said softly. "Education or anything education-related is what mattered most to him, and that influenced me a lot. I started school nearly a year earlier than most kids; it just worked out that way. Then I skipped a grade, finished college in three years by taking summer classes, and got my graduate degree pretty quickly. So, I was only twenty-four when I earned my doctorate. He wanted me to be a professor, always saw that as the ultimate badge of honor, as proof that one is learned."

"And what did you want?" he asked, taking her hand.

"I taught for a couple of years, but research was my real passion.

Research wasn't abstract to me; it was more of a mission to learn everything I could about the arts in the hope of shaping education policy and practices, influencing the flow of research dollars, that kind of thing. Anyway, when my dad retired, that workaholic city boy shocked the hell out of everyone by moving to Florida. Now he spends his days lounging by the pool and shaking down the other seniors in his community in highly questionable card games."

Rye laughed, genuinely enthralled by Dee's telling of her life story. "And your mother?"

"The funny thing is, my dad fancies himself an intellectual, but my mother was just the opposite. Never finished high school. When they met, she was working at the cosmetics counter of a department store. He was trying to buy a tie, but the line in the men's department was too long, so a salesclerk sent him over to cosmetics. He says it was love at first sight; she was very beautiful. I always thought she looked like Glinda the Good Witch, but maybe that's just because she seemed magical to me. Blonde hair, blue eyes. We don't look alike, obviously. I'm so ordinary compared to her."

"Sweetheart, there is nothing ordinary about you," he said. "You have the most beautiful brown eyes I've ever seen."

She glanced down. "Anyway, she died when I was ten. One day she didn't feel well, and before we knew it, she was gone."

"I'm so sorry," he said, rubbing her hand.

"Thank you. Studying was a good distraction, which is probably why I finished school so quickly. I think it's also why I turned to art—to escape, to find beauty. I buried myself in novels and books of poetry, took refuge in movie theaters, crawled into the sounds coming through my headphones, and I wrote. The outer world could be heartbreakingly disappointing, so I guess I turned to my inner world. Does that make sense?"

He looked at her with an expression of deep understanding, of knowing. "I've never heard anyone say it that way before, but it's like you put my feelings into words. In my own way, I think I did the same thing, hiding in story worlds even though the whole world was watching." He paused and said, "I lost my mother too."

"I know. It must have been awful. How old were you?"

"Eight."

"I'm so sorry," she said, reaching up and stroking his cheek tenderly.

"It was a crazed fan. My parents had been at an awards show. My father wanted to go to an after-party, but my mother was tired, so she had the driver take her home. It wasn't until he got home in the wee hours that he realized she had never made it. That morning, he learned she had been abducted. Cameras everywhere, and yet no one saw what happened. They found her the next day. He had . . . He had shot her."

"It's just horrific. I'm so sorry."

"The worst part was that the media got hold of the crime scene photos. I had to see it splashed all over television, newspapers, and magazines for what seemed like an eternity. I'm sure the adults tried to shield me from it, but it was everywhere. Frederick and Rebecca Field had been anointed Hollywood's golden couple. Her murder shook up the whole town. They say it's the day Tinseltown tarnished. To this day, I still get asked about it."

"People can be so insensitive."

"In some ways, it really made me put up walls. It's made me defensive with the press, which is not great in my line of work. Also . . ."

"What?" she asked gently.

"Because my mother died when and the way she did, my parents became frozen in the collective imaginary as the paradigmatic Hollywood couple." He shook his head and sighed. "But it wasn't true. They were having horrible problems. My dad was cheating. Even at my age, I knew they were heading for a divorce. It's been tough to keep up that mythology all these years."

"I bet," she said, reaching for his hand.

"He's had a million girlfriends and I have a slew of half siblings, but I think it's why he never married again: he didn't want to shatter the illusion. He lives in the shadow of what the world wanted them to be."

"Are you close to him?"

He nodded. "Probably not in the way you are with your father, though. We don't see each other as much as I'd like because we're both usually off filming something." He paused and ran his hand through his hair. "He's a giant in the industry, even to this day. When you said it's a lot to live up to with your father, I understood. I've always felt the same way. Even though we're both actors, I have always tried to find my own way. I'm proud to be his son, but I needed to be my own man."

She smiled. "I get it. My father offered to publish my first book. It was pretty controversial and no one wanted to touch it, but fail or succeed, I needed to do it myself. He gave me such grief when I finally found an agent and signed with a different publisher, but secretly, I think he respected it. I'm sure your father feels the same way. You're enormously talented. He must be proud of you." She paused and squeezed his hand, rubbing the back of it with her thumb. "What was your mother like?"

"Talented. Beautiful. Kind. She had the most wonderful smile. I know her mostly through her films."

"I wish I had something like that. My mother's voice . . ." She looked down. He caressed her arm and she continued. "I can't remember it. It's strange because I remember countless moments together, small details, things she said to me, but I lost her voice."

"Remembering the love is what really matters."

The conversation continued, and soon two hours had passed. "You sure you don't want this?" Rye asked, picking up the last french fry. "It's cold and greasy."

She laughed. "It's all you."

He threw away the takeout wrappers and put the dishes in the sink. Dee came up behind him and wrapped her arms around him. He turned to face her, put his hands on her hips, and they stared into each other's eyes.

"What are you thinking?" he asked.

"You're so confident, in a good way. I like that about you."

"Sweetheart, I feel like a schoolboy who is standing next to his dream girl, just hoping not to embarrass himself."

She blushed.

"You're someone I definitely want to impress. Tell me I haven't blown my chance."

"Just the opposite," she assured him.

He smiled and kissed her forehead, lingering in the embrace for a long moment. "How about we turn this takeout into dinner and dancing? Give me a second," he said as he went to turn on some music. The romantic sounds of piano and strings drifted in from speakers hidden in the ceiling. He returned and said, "Come here," taking her hand. He held one hand and placed another on the small of her back. She put her hand on his bicep and they slowly swayed, their bodies pressed together, melting into each other. She'd only known him for a few hours, but the connection was undeniable. She felt safe in his arms, like she'd always belonged there. Suddenly, he wrapped his arms around her and quickly whirled her around. As their bodies slowed, she giggled. "I told you, I like surprises," he said, brushing her hair out of her face. "Do you want to go to my room?"

She nodded.

He took her hand and led her upstairs to his bedroom. She gently ran her fingers along his arm. He cupped her face in his hands and kissed her softly. Gingerly, he untucked her shirt from her jeans and pulled it over her head, her hair falling in long cascades. She pulled off his shirt and they started kissing passionately, running their fingers through each other's hair. He stopped, caught his breath, and whispered, "I don't want to screw this up."

"You're not. I want you so badly. Be with me."

He picked her up, carried her to the bed, and gently laid her down. They took off the rest of their clothes and made love intimately, their eyes locked. After, they lay side by side, tenderly kissing.

"Sweetheart, I could get used to that," he said. "I feel so good with you, I can't even describe it."

She looked down.

He touched her chin and raised her face to meet his gaze. "You are so special, Dee. Please don't leave. Stay with me."

"Hold me," she whispered, turning around, her back against his chest. He wrapped his strong arms around her, and they fell asleep.

3

THE NEXT MORNING, DEE OPENED HER EYES, STILL BUR-rowed in Rye's warm embrace. She lightly touched the tips of her fingers to the tips of his.

"Hey, sweetheart. Good morning."

"Good morning," she said.

He squeezed her and asked, "Did you sleep well?"

"Yeah. You?"

"Never better. It feels so good, holding you like this," he said, kissing the back of her head. "Don't move," he instructed, slipping out of bed and heading to the bathroom. She admired his body as he walked away.

He returned a few minutes later in boxer shorts, sat on the edge of the bed beside her, and handed her an oversized Metallica T-shirt. He kissed her forehead and said, "I thought you might want to throw this on; I can get you something else if you prefer. I left a new tooth-brush on the bathroom counter for you."

"Thanks," she replied, sitting up and slipping the shirt on. "Ooh, it's soft."

"It's my favorite one," he said, pulling her long hair out of the back of the shirt.

"Did you ever see their performance of 'Nothing Else Matters' with a symphony? It's beautiful. I love when art is reimagined, taken to a new place."

He smiled. "I'll have to see that."

"Let me go brush my teeth and wash my face," she said, getting out of bed. A few minutes later as she was returning, she noticed an acoustic guitar in the corner of the bedroom. "Do you play?"

He nodded. "Bring it over."

She grabbed the guitar and hopped back into bed, propping herself up against pillows next to Rye. He started strumming. "Here, I'll do one you like," he said, and he began playing a stripped-down version of "Nothing Else Matters." He stared straight into her eyes as he sang the ballad. As he sat with Dee, he understood the lyrics for the first time. When he finished the song, he put the guitar on the floor beside the bed.

"That gave me goose bumps," she said.

He kissed her lovingly. "You're so sweet."

"How long have you been playing?"

"Since I was a kid. I've lugged that thing to every film and television set I've ever been on. Acting for the screen involves a lot of waiting. I'm usually stuck in my trailer for hours on end, so I practice. I write a little too, have a notebook full of songs or potential songs. I'll show you my music room later if you want to see it." He laughed and said, "I have a little addiction to collecting guitars."

She smiled.

"Music is the only thing I love as much as acting."

"You're really good. You have a great voice, super sexy."

He blushed, suddenly unable to meet her eyes.

"Did you ever think about pursuing music for real?"

He squirmed a little and eventually said, "Yeah, I'd love to put a little band together and record some stuff with this producer friend of mine, maybe even do some live shows. It's just . . ."

"What?" she asked, placing a supportive hand on his thigh.

"There's such a stigma about actors who try to do music. People think it's easy for celebrities."

"Rye, come on. If it's not easy for you, who is it easy for?"

He looked at her like he didn't know how to respond.

"I just mean it's hard for anyone to make art, to make themselves vulnerable in that way, and put themselves out there. It takes courage. Most people who do it have a lot more riding on it and have no safety net. At the end of the day, you're still a hugely successful guy with more money than you'll ever need. Nothing will change that."

"I've been talking to my close friends about this for years, and no one has ever said anything like that to me. Uh, thank you for putting me in my place."

She bit her lip and quietly said, "That's not how I meant it."

He met her gaze and caressed the side of her face. "No, I mean it. Thank you."

"Life is short. If you want to make music, do it. It doesn't matter what anyone else thinks. Besides, any critic who can't understand an artist who is inclined to be creative in more than one area isn't a very deep thinker."

He laughed.

"I'd love to hear some of your original songs."

He pressed his mouth gently to hers. "I would love to play something for you, but right now I'm distracted by how pretty you are in the morning light," he said, tucking a strand of hair behind her ear.

She smiled, pulled her shirt off, and they tumbled onto the bed and made love.

"Are you sure I can't help?" Dee asked.

Rye walked over with the coffee pot, filled her mug, and kissed the top of her head. "You just sit and relax. This is the only thing I can make on my own. Spicy or not spicy?"

"Spicy, always."

"A woman after my own heart."

She giggled. "I should really check my messages," she said as she retrieved her phone from her handbag. "Ah, only a dozen text messages from Sara and Troy. They're the friends I ditched last night."

"Were they upset?"

"No, although Sara thought I was out of my mind to leave with you. She's kind of uptight—well, that sounds unflattering . . . cautious. She's a little cautious."

"Would she have been against you leaving with anyone, or should I take it personally?"

Dee laughed. "Maybe a little of both. We met in graduate school, she's very studious, brainy. It's funny because she's a professor at UCLA, teaches film studies of all things, but she's not so keen on actors, at least not the famous ones. Every year she gets invited to film festivals—Cannes, Venice, Berlin. She spends all her time there attending screenings, but she never goes to any of the parties. Celebrity offends her."

"And you?"

"No, not at all, but to be honest, I'm not enamored by it. Fame seems a bit silly to me. Being an actor is great and I respect it, but I don't see much difference between the A-listers and the unknowns. It's about the work." She paused for a moment to consider her words. "Besides, if you really think about how our culture places value, it seems to me like the most celebrated people should be the ones curing diseases, healing the sick, freeing the oppressed, teaching the young, protecting the country, and so on, not those who are lucky enough to spend their life making art and entertainment. Our value system is a little off."

He huffed. "I don't disagree with you."

"I don't want to give you a bad impression of Sara. She's super smart and a loyal friend. You'd like her, I think. You just have to consider where she's coming from; academia is a snake pit, kind of like our government."

Rye laughed.

"Oh, you laugh, but trust me, I know. Aside from Hollywood or Washington, DC, there's nothing more hierarchical and elitist than academia. It's kind of like high school, but with funding wars. A few people are elevated to the popular crew, a couple of whom are anointed prom king and queen, and everyone else has to pretend to be happy for them while they work their behinds off for no recognition, substandard treatment, and little pay. Sara's always been a worker bee. She sees parallels between Hollywood and academia, that's all. Makes her suspicious of those who have 'made it.'"

Rye laughed. "What about your friend Troy?"

"Troy has a major crush on you. I told him he's not your type," she said with a laugh. "He's all heart. You'd like him. Apparently, he fell in lust with your character on *The Mission*, which I must confess, I've never seen."

"Really?"

"Yeah, sorry. I don't watch much TV. I'm more of a reader."

"Don't be sorry. It's refreshing, actually. I played that role for so long that I worry people see me as him, that they can't tease us apart. I couldn't be more different from Bruce Jones. It can make it hard to meet people, which is probably why I tend to stay in my little bubble and date actresses."

"What about your friends last night? Were they upset you missed the show?"

"I told them I met someone special. They could see it in my eyes."

She blushed.

He walked over and said, "Huevos rancheros with hot sauce for the beautiful girl," as he placed their dishes on the table.

"This looks great. Thank you."

"My pleasure," he said, dropping into the adjacent chair. "Do you have any plans today? Do you have to work?"

"No plans. Working for myself has its advantages. You?"

He shook his head. "I just wrapped up a project. The next big one doesn't start for a while. Spend the day with me."

"I'd love to."

"Wow, you weren't kidding when you said you had a guitar addiction," Dee observed, looking around the room littered with guitars. "What kind of music do you like to listen to?"

"Everything. Rock, alternative, country."

"What about the music you write?"

"Well, since I've never recorded any of it, I'm not really sure. In my mind, it's kind of Americana." She sat on the plush couch and Rye handed her a black, leather-bound notebook. "These are the songs I've jotted down over the years," he said, taking the seat beside her.

"May I?" she asked.

"Of course."

She opened the notebook and started reading his handwritten lyrics, flipping from page to page.

"I must admit that I'm kind of nervous all of a sudden," he said. "I've never shared these with anyone."

She smiled. "Thank you for sharing them with me." She continued reading and said, "You're a great writer. They're beautiful. There's a simplicity to them that I like."

He smiled. "Those are about heartache."

"This one's funny," she said, laughing.

"My life has been pretty wild. I have some good stories that I've tried to capture in song. Always thought those would be fun to play in a live show."

"Will you sing one for me?" she asked.

He grabbed an acoustic guitar and played her a song. When he finished, she tucked her feet under her and said, "Do another."

For the next two hours, he played his original songs and a few covers. They sat together marking up his lyrics, Dee offering several suggestions for a word or new phrasing here and there, which he scribbled down. "You're so clever with language," he remarked.

"Poetry forces you to be precise, that's all."

He put the guitar and notebook down, kissed her, and said, "Do you feel like watching a movie? I have popcorn and loads of snacks."

She nodded.

"What's your favorite film?" he asked.

"*Cinema Paradiso*, the director's cut."

He smiled. "That's one of my favorites too. What do you like about it?"

"It celebrates the magic of movies, of art, and the magic of true love." He took her hand and massaged her fingers. "Of course, the ending wrecks me, when he watches all the kissing scenes his friend had saved and edited together. Makes me cry for days."

He kissed her softly.

"What was that for?"

"You're just so sweet I can barely stand it," he said. "Come on, let's get the popcorn."

They watched movies all day, snuggling together on the couch. Just as it started to get dark, Rye said, "How about we go for a swim?"

"Your pool is amazing," Dee said as Rye slipped his hands around her waist. "You know, I've never been skinny-dipping before. This is my first time."

"Really?" he asked.

"Uh-huh. I told you, I'm shy."

He kissed the tip of her nose. "Well, I did offer to loan you a bathing suit."

"Yeah, wearing something one of your exes left behind didn't really appeal to me."

"Fair enough," he said with a chuckle. "Besides, you're beautiful. You should never cover up this body with clothes."

She looked down, blushing. "I'm sure the women you've been with have been perfect."

"Sweetheart, there's not a single thing about you I would change. You have these perfect, delicate breasts," he said, running his hand down the sides of her torso, "and you're so petite I can pick you up just like this." He pulled her up, and she flung her legs around his waist. "And don't even get me started on this," he said as he began nibbling on her earlobe. "Or this," he continued, kissing her neck. "I can't seem to get enough of you."

"Make love with me," she whispered.

He carried her out of the pool and sat down on a chaise lounge with her in his lap. They made love passionately, kissing and running their hands through each other's wet hair until they screamed together in ecstasy. Afterward, he lay down and gently pulled Dee next to his still-quivering body. He touched his forehead to hers and said, "We have such a strong connection. It's not just physical; there's this closeness between us, like we've known each other forever. I can't even explain how I feel about you."

"Me too," she said softly. "Can we just lie here quietly for a little while?"

He kissed her and wrapped his arms around her. She rested her head on his chest, and they relaxed in each other's embrace. Eventually, Rye said, "I'm a terrible host. I should feed you something. How about we get dinner delivered?"

Dee walked out of the bathroom, towel-drying her hair, wearing Rye's T-shirt again. "You are so sexy," he said, walking over and kissing her. "Come on, the food is waiting. I poured myself a whiskey and opened a great bottle of wine for you."

"There's nothing like eating Chinese food out of the containers," Dee said, maneuvering the last shrimp dumpling into her mouth. She put the chopsticks down and said, "Really reminds me of New York."

"You never told me why you moved to sunny California."

She smiled. "I spent a lot of time here when I was a kid. One of my dad's oldest friends lives in LA. We usually visited at least once or twice a year. Then, after my mom died . . ."

He took her hand and looked at her tenderly.

"This friend knew it was a lot for my dad to be on his own with me, so he'd fly me out to LA for all my school breaks. He and his wife were so good to me; they took me to the beach, to see all the sights, on studio tours and to movie sets, which was magical for a kid. Mostly, I spent hours relaxing by their pool, just reading books. His wife would cook some of my mother's old recipes, just for me. Their house always smelled like her. I cherished those visits."

He absentmindedly played with her fingers while she spoke. "Anyway, I've always felt a connection to LA. Sara, that friend from graduate school I told you about, also lives here. About five years ago,

I bought a place in Malibu, and I split my time between California and New York. I can work from anywhere. A couple of months ago, I made the leap and moved here full-time." She looked down and said, "If I tell you the reason I moved here, I'm afraid of what you'll think."

He massaged her hand and said, "It's okay, I promise. Tell me."

"I was about to turn forty, which was always a scary age to me. My mother died when she was forty." He interlaced his fingers with hers and she continued, "As my birthday was approaching, it hit me pretty hard and I stopped to take stock of my life. I don't want to call it a midlife crisis or anything too dramatic, but I examined my life and realized something wasn't right. I'm a little embarrassed to say I wasn't really happy, or at least not as happy as I felt I should be."

"Why are you embarrassed about that?"

"I'm enormously privileged. I have a career doing what I love. Between what I've earned and what my father gave me after he sold his business, I'm financially set for life. Most people have to get up every day and go to work at jobs they don't even enjoy, just to survive. I'm blessed, and that comes with a unique kind of privilege. When you don't have to worry about the basics, all that remains are experiences. Life is a string of experiences. You have to think about what they bring you and what they bring others, whether it's how you make someone feel, a memory you leave with them, or what you create that will be left behind, like a piece of scholarship, a poem, a film, or a song."

He huffed. "You've done it again."

"What?"

"Put my feelings into words. I've been thinking about this my whole adult life, but never as insightfully as that. I know how lucky I am."

She smiled. "There was this guy, Russell Winthrop. He's an

investment banker. We'd been together for over two years. One day, I was in his apartment, looking for a sweater to borrow, when I accidentally stumbled upon an engagement ring. My friends told me he was planning to propose on my birthday. And I knew," she said, shaking her head, "I knew my answer would be no. So, I broke it off with him."

"Why didn't you want to marry him?"

"Right after I finished graduate school, I was with this guy, Jett Reed. We met by chance in a coffee shop. I was reading a book for a class I was teaching, and he asked me about it. Then he offered to sketch me. He's an artist. We fell in love. Other than a couple of semi-serious boyfriends I had in school, he was really my first major relationship. I thought he was the one. We lived together for a couple of years, and were on and off for a bit after that. I've given him money a few times over the years, bailing him out of stuff. He always had a wild, reckless streak—drinks too much, does other stuff that messes him up, gets in his own way. I was ambitious. I really wanted to do something big in the world, and at some point, I knew it wouldn't be possible with him. That kind of relationship drags you down. Even though it was my choice, I was heartbroken. It was an impossible choice because I truly believe in following your heart, but . . ."

"Sometimes we all have to make hard decisions."

"After that, I focused on my career. Eventually I started dating again, but nothing lasted long. When I met Russell, he was everything that Jett wasn't: stable, ambitious, safe. You know, good on paper. Since I had been burned, that was attractive to me. We both had serious careers, so it seemed to make sense." She sighed and shrugged. "But you can't lie to your own heart. When I saw that diamond ring, I knew I didn't love him. That sort of sent me into a tailspin, wondering how I ended up in a two-year relationship with a man I didn't love. What else was I missing?" He kissed her hand. She continued, "Worst of all, I began to wonder if it's even possible to have passion for your work and passionate love at the same time."

He squeezed her hand and said, "An extraordinary life."

She smiled. They stared at each other for a long moment before she said, "Los Angeles was always a respite from dark times, a place of dreams, so I sold my loft in Tribeca, followed the yellow brick road, and here I am."

"I think that was brave."

She smiled again and took another sip of her wine, warmth and relaxation spreading through her limbs. "What about you? How come you're still unattached?"

"I got married young, when I was twenty-one. Sascha, my ex, is an actress. We were in love, but I think it was that kind of puppy love you have when you're young and don't fully know yourself yet. I meant it to be forever, but life happened. Being an actor requires a certain kind of selfishness. In some ways, the world revolves around your schedule. I was constantly away, for months on end. It's a strange thing to tell your wife, 'Hey, I'm doing a movie, I'll be gone for three months,' but that's the reality of my life. The truth is that I was lazy, took her for granted, didn't do the work that it takes to have a successful marriage. We had been living completely separate lives when I met Krysta Dunn on a movie set. We fell in love. By the time our wedding day arrived, she had become incredibly famous and we were under tremendous scrutiny. The media decided that we were Hollywood's next golden couple."

"Was that hard for you, because of your parents?" she asked.

He smiled and stroked her hair. "No one has ever asked me that. Yes, it was hard. I felt like we were stepping into cursed territory, but I truly loved her and just tried to focus on that. In the end, she decided it was all too much for her. She wanted to focus on her career without the added pressure of a high-profile relationship. I was utterly heart-broken. It was difficult to grieve the end of our relationship while the media ran wild with the story. Because she was America's sweetheart, they naturally cast me as the villain, made up all kinds of stories to justify her leaving me." He stopped and shook his head. "The sad thing is, in the end, I lived up to it. Figured if everyone thought I was the bad guy, I should at least have some fun. Went on a pretty big bender, drinking too much, partying with inappropriate women, embarrassing myself publicly, trying to forget. Eventually I got myself under control. Not long after, I started working on *The Mission* and my life became fourteen-hour workdays for the next twelve years."

"And your personal life?" she asked.

"I dated a few women seriously. I was with my last girlfriend, Lucy, for four years. We lived together. She wanted to get married and I didn't. It had nothing to do with my feelings for her; I had just decided marriage wasn't for me. I hadn't been good at it. Lucy pushed me to make it official, so we broke up. When her ultimatum failed, she tried to reconcile, but I knew we would end up right back where we were, so I let her go so she could find what she really wanted and deserved."

She reached out and put her hand on his cheek. "You are so often portrayed as some kind of rebellious bachelor, but all I see is a sweet, kind man with boyhood heartache in his eyes."

"I don't open up to most people this way."

"Me neither."

He stood up, kissed her head, and said, "I'm going to clean up so I can take you to bed. All I want is to feel you in my arms."

"Okay, but tomorrow you have to take me home, at least so I can change my outfit," she replied with a smile.

"If you're not busy, maybe I could bring an overnight bag and stay the night. I'm not ready to let you go, and I'd love to see your place."

"I was hoping you'd say that."

4

"RIGHT ON THE PACIFIC COAST HIGHWAY—THIS IS A
hell of an address," Rye said as he parked the car.

"Don't get me wrong, I love New York, but it's a concrete jungle.
When I decided to buy a place in LA, there was nowhere else I could
imagine. Living on the beach is such a dream. There's nothing like the
sea air. It's great for my writing too. Come on," she said as they got out
of the car. With the Pacific Ocean just beyond her property line, she led
him into her modern, two-floor house. "You give up some space for the
location, but it's more than I need and the views and beach access make
it worth it. You can see the ocean as soon as you walk inside."

"That view is killer," he agreed.

"Just drop your bag there for now."

He set his bag down and looked around. "Wood floors and light
gray walls, it seems we have the same taste. This place is beautiful."

"Thank you."

"Wow, this is a great installation," he said, admiring a series of
framed photographs on the living room wall. "I love black-and-white
photography."

She smiled. "A friend of mine took those. So, you can see the first
floor is all open concept. Upstairs, there are a couple of bedrooms
and my office. The best part of this place is the deck, which is where I
spend most of my time," she explained, taking his hand and leading
him outside.

He wrapped his arms around her and they stood still and silent, mesmerized by the cobalt sea. Eventually, Dee said, "I should really go change into some fresh clothes. What do you feel like doing today?"

"Anything. I just want to be with you."

She glanced down, he pulled her chin back up to meet his gaze, and they kissed.

"If we stay here, I think we'll end up in bed all day," she said. "How about we go for a hike?"

He kissed her softly and said, "Sounds perfect."

"Maybe after, we can stop at the farmers' market. We can pick some food up for tonight. I'd love to make you dinner."

He smiled at her affectionately. "That's sweet."

"Can I get you anything while you wait?" she asked.

"Another kiss," he replied, leaning forward and pressing his mouth to hers.

"Feel free to poke around. I'll be ready soon."

"It's such a beautiful day," Dee remarked as they wandered hand in hand through the farmers' market.

"That was a breathtaking hiking trail," Rye said. "It's one of the great things about living in California; you can get a good workout without being stuck in the gym."

"I go running on the beach most mornings. So much of my work life is spent indoors, so I try to soak up the fresh air whenever possible."

"Me too," he said, lifting her hand to his lips and kissing it.

Dee noticed people recognizing Rye, even though he was wearing aviator sunglasses and a baseball cap. They walked past a few young women who looked at him with giddiness, whispered to each other, and then giggled hello.

"Hi," he replied.

"I loved *The Mission*," one of them said. "Best show ever."

"Thank you so much," he casually replied, and they strolled on.

"You're very kind to your fans," Dee said.

"They let me do what I love. I'm grateful to them beyond words."

She smiled, more enamored with him by the minute. They arrived at a butcher stand, and Dee asked, "So, what should we pick up for dinner? What do you like?"

"I'm easy. Whatever you feel like."

"Do you like chicken?" she asked.

"Yes."

"Okay." She turned to the vendor and said, "A pound of boneless, skinless chicken thighs, please." While they waited for their order, she turned to Rye and said, "You deserve a home-cooked meal. I'm guessing it's been a while."

"You're so sweet," he said. He took the bag of chicken from the vendor and thanked him. "Where to next?"

"Produce. I say after we get the food home, we lounge around on the beach."

"Sounds perfect."

"You have great taste in music. Your record collection is awesome. All the classics and the harder-to-find stuff," Rye said, pulling another album off the shelf.

"I don't care much about material possessions, but I do love art, books, and music. You've been an excellent deejay. I totally appreciate the ease of digital music, but nothing beats the sound of vinyl."

"Agreed. You sure I can't help?" he asked.

"Nope. It'll be ready in a minute. You can open the wine if you like."

"I noticed you have a lot of foreign language albums," he remarked.

"Yeah. Most people around here seem to think that all music comes from the US or the UK, but there's so much incredible music created around the world. Completely different sounds and structures. The more you experience art from different places, the more it opens your mind. I buy local music from each new place I visit in my travels. Most of my friends are artists, and they often bring me things too. I'll play you something special later if you want."

"I would love that. The wine is poured," Rye said.

"Here you go," Dee said, setting down the plates. "Braised chicken in a fresh apricot glaze on crispy saffron rice with sautéed swiss chard and kale."

"It looks like art. I'm impressed," he gushed, pulling out her chair.

"Cooking relaxes me. It's especially nice to make something for someone you care about."

"I'd like to propose a toast," he said, raising his glass. "To new beginnings."

"To new beginnings," she repeated, clinking her glass to his.

They began eating. Rye took a bite and raved, "Wow, this is amazing."

"I'm glad you like it." She took a sip of wine and said, "I better not drink too much. I'm so relaxed from lying on the beach, but I don't want to pass out. The sea air makes me sleepy."

"Sweetheart, I want to say something to you, but I don't want to freak you out."

"Well, now you kinda have to say it or I will be freaked out."

He laughed and took her hand. "At the end of the day, when we were lying quietly together on that lounge chair and you were curled up in my arms, it just felt so right, so easy. This means something to me. You mean something to me. I just want to make sure you know that."

She caressed his fingers and said, "I feel the same way."

"Tomorrow night I have to go to a business dinner. I'm hoping you'll join me. It will be all couples. I was planning to go alone, but then I met you."

She smiled. "I'd be happy to go with you. What's the dinner for?"

"An upcoming film project I'm working on with Billy Sumner and Grey Hewson."

"Billy Sumner? Oh, do you mean William Sumner?"

"Yeah, but friends call him Billy. He's actually one of my closest friends. We met when we were teenagers and were just starting out. We still pinch ourselves that we somehow both made it. Anyway, it's a terrific script, a drama based on a true story about a murder in a small town. I'm playing the lead detective, Billy's the victim's father, and Grey's the bad guy. We've all wanted to work together for a while, but we've been waiting for the right project. This is a big one to me. We're all producing too, and we have a major studio backing us."

"Sounds great," she said.

"The meeting is with Oliver Spence," Rye added.

"The British director?"

"We're trying to convince him to come on board."

"He's terrific. He has such a unique, honest way of telling stories. Clean, that's it. It's a clean, modern sensibility."

Rye smiled. "We think so too. He's the hottest director on the scene right now, so he can afford to pick and choose his projects. He's very selective. We're hoping a dinner will seal the deal."

"I read an interview he gave recently. He talked about how much his body of work means to him, you know, what he'll leave behind. He wants to make exceptional, timeless films—cinema, not just movies. I think he has an artist's soul."

Rye squeezed her hand and said, "See? How could I possibly go to this dinner without you?"

She blushed. "I'm sure you'd do just fine."

"Then I'll revise my statement. How could I possibly go anywhere at all without you?"

After loading the dishwasher, Dee was drying her hands when Rye came up behind her, moved her hair aside, and kissed her neck. "Thank you again for that wonderful dinner."

"My pleasure."

"I was thinking—I played you some of my music. Would you read me some of your poetry? I'd love to hear it."

"That's sweet. Sure. Come on," she said, taking his hand and guiding him upstairs to her office.

She walked over to her desk while he perused her bookshelves. "Deanna Schwartz," he said as he pulled one of her books off the shelf. "That's your full name?"

"Uh-huh," she said.

"*New York Times* best seller, wow," he said. "I didn't realize. I mean, you didn't mention . . ."

"Those things don't matter to me," she replied. "Accolades don't change what's on the pages of the book. That's all that matters. God help any artist who cares about sales or reviews."

He huffed. She pulled a notebook out of her desk drawer and said, "Come to my room and we can get cozy in bed. I'll read you some of the poems I've been working on lately."

He turned to follow her when he noticed a box of plaques on the floor in the corner of the room. "What are those?" he asked.

"Nothing important. Come on," she said, taking his hand and pulling him along behind her.

They crawled into bed. Rye propped up some pillows, extended his arm, and Dee burrowed into him. She opened her notebook and read several poems.

Rye laughed hysterically. "You're so funny. Those are great. I've never heard anything like them. Ballsy as hell, for lack of a better word."

She smiled. "I like to have fun with my writing. Thought you'd appreciate some of the lighter, edgier ones. There are some more serious ones too. Here," she said, and she read a couple more.

"My God, you're really talented. Those are absolutely beautiful."

"Thank you. I've written a bunch about my mother, about the hole she left behind. I know it's close to home for you too, so if . . ."

He pulled her tighter against him and said, "Please, I'd love to hear."

"This one's called 'Over Every Rainbow.' It's sort of a chronological story from a child's perspective through to adulthood, about how you look for beauty everywhere to fill the void, the loneliness of a grief that will never pass." She took a deep breath and began reading the poem.

He sniffled as she read it. When she finished, she put the notebook down and looked up at him. Tears slid down his cheeks. She used her fingers to gently wipe away the salty water. "Thank you for sharing that with me," he mumbled through his tears. She held his face and kissed him softly. He caressed her arms, then her face, and then started pulling off her clothes. They made love slowly, their eyes locked on each other.

They slept until nearly eleven o'clock the next morning, entangled in each other's embrace.

"Good morning, sweetheart," he said.

"Good morning."

He touched her cheek, stared adoringly into her eyes, and said, "I . . . I . . ."

"What is it?" she asked softly, tracing his jawline with her finger.

"I never expected this. This is just very special," he said.

She smiled. "Rye, the way I feel about you, well, I don't even have the words. It's everything."

He caressed her face.

"Let's take a shower and then I'll make some coffee," she said.

A little while later, they were getting ready to take their coffee onto the deck when the doorbell rang. "Oh, shit," Dee mumbled. "It's Sunday, isn't it?"

"Yeah, who are you expecting?" Rye asked.

"I have a standing weekly brunch with Sara and Troy. I've been so blissfully preoccupied with you that I completely forgot."

She answered the door and Troy came bounding in, Sara following. "Hi, hi," he said cheerily, kissing her on both cheeks. "There's a Porsche outside, and . . ." He stopped midsentence when he saw Ryder. "Ah, that explains it," he said, throwing Dee a mischievous glance.

"Troy, Sara, this is Rye Field," she said.

"Nice to meet you both," Rye said, extending his hand.

"Likewise," Troy replied, looking him up and down as they shook hands.

Sara placed a pastry box on the counter and shook Rye's hand. She turned to Dee and said, "If we're interrupting . . ."

"Not at all," Rye insisted. He turned to Dee and kissed her

forehead. "I really should get going anyway. I need to stop by Billy's to strategize for the meeting tonight."

"You're welcome to join us for brunch. Please stay," Dee replied.

"Yes, absolutely. The more the merrier," Troy said.

Rye smiled and took Dee's hand. "Thank you, but you all go ahead and have your plans. Let's do it another time. I'll just go grab my things."

He walked out of the room and Troy stared Dee down, his eyes so wide they were nearly popping out of his head. "Damn, he's fine," he said softly. "Did he come over last night, or . . ."

"We've been together since we left the bar Thursday night."

"Well, brunch is certainly looking up. I was afraid we'd be stuck listening to Sara complain about her latest department meeting or her students' eternal complacency. Instead, you can regale us with stories of your wild weekend with everyone's favorite action hero."

Dee giggled and Sara shot him the side-eye.

Rye returned, sunglasses on and overnight bag in hand. He gently touched Dee's wrist and said, "Thank you for everything. I'll pick you up at seven." He kissed her more reservedly than before, but no less intimately. He turned to the others and said, "It was nice to meet you both. Enjoy your brunch." He kissed Dee again and left.

5

"WELL, I'M IMPRESSED BY HOW QUICKLY YOU WHIPPED up that frittata, considering that you obviously forgot we were coming," Troy said as they all sat down at the outdoor dining table.

Dee giggled.

"This is just so unlike you," Sara remarked, cutting her muffin into equal quarters.

"I know. This whole thing has been unlike me. I even went skinny-dipping in his pool. That was a first."

"Long overdue, if you ask me," Troy said, raising his mimosa and winking. "Tell us everything. What's he like in bed? He seems like a take-control type of guy. Was it dirty, in that fabulous, morally ambiguous kind of way?"

"I don't want to hear about the sex," Sara groaned.

"Then cover your ears," Troy countered.

Dee smiled, looked down, and bit her lip.

"Wow, it must have really been something if you're getting flustered even with us," Troy said. He threw his napkin down on the table with decisive, dramatic flair. "That's it. Tell us everything."

"It was magical. We have a connection that's hard to explain. I feel so close to him."

"Really?" Sara asked.

"Yeah. He loves art as much as I do. We watched movies, he played a bunch of music—he's a guitarist and he writes his own songs.

He has a super sexy voice. I read him my poetry." She paused for a moment and then continued, "And it's not just common interests. We fundamentally understand each other. We both lost our mothers when we were young. It's something you can't understand unless you've been through it."

"I can see how that would be bonding," Sara said, beginning to sound more sympathetic.

"He's not like what you might think, not at all how the tabloids make him out to be. He's sweet and gentle, confident yet vulnerable. He's definitely outgoing and you know what I'm like, but when we were together, I felt bolder. I got the feeling that he felt more settled or something, centered. We were both more ourselves somehow. I don't know how to explain it. We just fit together so naturally. When I was in his arms, there's no other place I ever wanted to be."

"Wow. You never talk like this. Here I thought it was just a sex romp," Troy joked.

Dee giggled. "It's definitely more than that."

"He said he's picking you up later. Where are you going?" Sara asked.

"Dinner with his colleagues. He's making a film with some friends, and they're trying to woo Oliver Spence into directing it."

"Oliver Spence? Really?" Sara asked, her eyes lighting up. "He's a terrific director. I teach his work in my contemporary film studies course."

Dee smiled. "Yeah, I like his work too."

"Who else will be there?" Troy asked.

"Grey and Sloane Hewson and William Sumner and his wife."

"Hold, please. We've been here for half an hour. How is this the first we're hearing of this?" he replied.

"Sorry, you know the celebrity thing doesn't really register with me."

"Well, don't be so selfish. Think of your guests, Dee. We want *all* the gossip," Troy said.

"Speak for yourself," Sara replied.

Dee laughed.

"You do realize you're having dinner with the three biggest superheroes in the world? Before he turned all serious and thespian, Grey got his start doing those superhero movies. God, I can still picture him in that rubber suit with that impossibly rippled chest plate. You'll have to tell me if he looks that good in person," Troy said. Dee giggled and he continued, "And William Sumner starred in the biggest superhero movies of all time. That franchise has grossed billions. I wonder what it's like to have an action figure made in your likeness."

Suddenly, Sara put her fork down, looked at them conspiratorially, and said, "I must admit, I'd love to meet Sloane Hewson."

Troy's jaw dropped. "I'm so taken aback that I can't even come up with a zinger."

Dee shot him a look of admonishment. "I'm disappointed in you."

"She's been in great films, real art. Besides, she uses her platform to speak out on social justice issues. She's a humanitarian," Sara explained.

"Of course she is; it's the hottest trend this season. She wears it well," Troy joked.

Sara gave him a stern look and continued, "She cares about women's rights, Black Lives Matter, the plight of refugees, and on and on."

"Plus, she's gorgeous as fuck. Talk about a flawless complexion! Dee, ask her about her skincare routine," Troy said.

"Yeah, I'll be sure to work it into the dinner conversation in between business discussions," she replied with a laugh.

"So, what are you wearing tonight? After brunch, I say we try on everything in your wardrobe. Don't worry, I'll veto anything that doesn't make you look fabulous. You know me—I won't hold back," Troy said.

"No doubt."

"I'm thinking about that slinky black sleeveless jumpsuit you have with a pair of stilettos. Sexy and chic," Troy said. "Uh, hello? Do you hear me? Suddenly you're a million miles away."

"Black jumpsuit, uh-huh, sounds good," Dee said.

"What on earth are you thinking about?" Troy asked.

She smiled and said softly, "Him. I'm just thinking about him."

"Hey, buddy," Billy said, giving him a warm hug.

"Good to see you, man," Rye replied.

"The girls are playing out back. I told them not to get in the pool until I got there to supervise, but they are untrustworthy little terrors, so we better hustle. Come on."

As soon as they got outside, the eight-year-old twins ran over. "Daddy, Daddy, can we go swimming now?"

"Say hello to Rye," he replied.

"Hello to Rye," they said.

"Hey, there," Rye said, bending down to hug them. "You two got so big."

"Now, Daddy, can we *please* go in now? Pleeeeease?" they whined.

"Stay in the shallow end," he replied.

"Will you come in too?" they asked in unison.

"A little later. Now go on," he said.

Rye laughed as the girls skipped off.

"It isn't funny. They're seriously wearing me out," Billy said, dropping into a chair and tossing Rye a bottled water.

Rye took a seat and said, "If people only knew that the superhero who routinely saves the world from unspeakable doom is getting his ass whipped by a couple of little girls."

"Movie villains don't hold a candle to those two little monsters. Kids will seriously humble you."

Rye smiled. "You look good. How's Susan?"

"She's good. She had to run to the office, but she's looking forward to seeing you tonight. I spoke with Grey, and he's prepared to take the lead with Oliver. Grey's a master negotiator. No one's better at doing the dance and closing the deal. We will all need to focus on impressing Oliver to make this happen. He's the star tonight. What he wants, he gets."

"Got it. I figured that was the plan. Speaking of tonight, I changed the reservation to eight people. I'm bringing someone."

"Ah, now I see why you came over instead of calling. And wait, what's that look on your face about?" Billy teased.

Rye blushed.

"Damn, brother, who is this girl? I don't remember seeing you turn that shade of red in a long time, if ever."

"Her name's Dee. We met by chance. She's just a regular girl, really sweet, gentle, and super smart. She's a scholar, has a doctorate, and she's written a bunch of books, best sellers. She is a champion for the arts. She's quiet, but when she has something to say, you want to listen to every word. And she's funny. I've never been with anyone like her."

Billy smiled. "I can't wait to meet her. Don't take this the wrong way, but you've basically been dating the same girl for decades. Always actresses or models, all a bit narcissistic, maybe a little superficial. Great to look at—I mean, Lucy's tight little dresses were something. Although at some point, do you really want to be *that* guy? You're getting older, buddy," he said with a laugh.

Rye shot him a look.

"Don't get me wrong, Lucy was very sweet. I liked her, everyone did, but she's someone who would spend her free time sitting in front of a mirror, examining her face from every angle and practicing posing in the hope that someday she'd be as famous as the guy on her arm. That's just who she is, whether you chose to see it or not."

Rye looked down, a little embarrassed.

"I know you two had a real relationship and cared deeply about each other. I don't mean to trivialize it, but the fact that you are Ryder Field mattered to her. If you were just you, do you really think she would have been with you? Every time you took her to an industry event, or the paparazzi snapped photos of you, or a fan asked you for an autograph, it was all over her face. She had that pretending-not-to-care look down pat, right as she'd strike a pose." Billy paused for a moment and said, "None of that even matters. It's just, she . . ."

"Please, tell me," Rye said.

"She was never going to make you anything other than what you already are. None of them were. And that's fine, if you're just looking for fun and someone pretty to tag along on the red carpet, but . . ."

"What? You can say whatever you're thinking."

"Look, it's like me and Susan. You know better than anyone what a mess I was before I met her. No amount of success in the public eye could change the reality that behind closed doors, I was a self-destructive little fuck. Money and fame just made it easier to stay that way. I had only been with women who were just like me in most ways, women who wouldn't challenge me or ask for too much. Sure, they were fun, but like beauty, fun fades. At some point, I realized I wanted to leave this world a better man than how I came into it. When I met Susan, I just got bowled over right away, and she was so different from the others—smart, stable, sincere, and she didn't take any of my shit. She didn't give a fuck who I was, saw through all the Hollywood bullshit. She's made me a better man. What I have now is a kind of partnership I never understood before; I thought I did, but I really didn't."

"You two are perfect for each other," Rye agreed.

"We have our moments, but I wouldn't want any of it without her."

Rye smiled. "I'm starting to understand what that might feel like. Dee and I have a lot in common, but our personalities are very different. She's shy, and you know me."

"Shy you ain't."

Rye laughed. "But we balance each other, like two pieces of a puzzle. Thought it the first night we met. And in her own sweet but direct way, she says things to me that no one else would. It's like she wants me to be happy and not stand in my own damn way." He paused and then timidly continued, "She thinks I should do something with my music. Record it, put it out there."

"As long as I've known you, you've been dragging around a guitar everywhere you go, like a damn shadow. It's about time someone convinced you to bite the bullet."

"Yeah, I know. Dee's so honest, so unfazed by the actor thing." He stopped and exhaled. "You know, I've never had any problems with women, always thought I was kind of smooth, but I actually get tongue-tied around her. She makes me feel bashful, like I just want to be smart enough to be with her."

"I feel that way every time Susan walks into the room, even after all these years."

Rye smiled, unable to keep the way he felt inside from spreading across his face.

"Damn, buddy. You're in deep."

"Yeah, I know."

"Daddy, Daddy," one of the girls called. "Are you coming in soon?"

"Soon," Billy replied.

"When I look at your girls, so carefree and innocent, it's hard to believe I was their age when I lost my mother."

"God, when I think about something like that happening to my girls, having to go through that kind of loss . . . I can't even imagine what it was like for you."

"Dee can. Her mother died when she was ten. It changes absolutely everything. People can have sympathy, but it's impossible to understand unless you've been through it."

"Rye, we've known each other for what, thirty-five years? Fuck, we're old." They both laughed. "I know you, buddy. People may think you're an open book, but there's another side that very few get to see. If this girl gets you, that sounds like something special."

"Can I tell you something you swear you'll never repeat if this thing blows up and ends tomorrow?"

"Of course."

"When we're together, I feel like I'm home."

Billy smiled. "Like I said, I can't wait to meet her. And here's a little unsolicited advice given in the spirit of friendship and without judgment." He took a dramatic pause and said, "Don't fuck it up. You've had the luxury to live an extraordinarily self-absorbed life. And God knows it's been a blast."

"It has indeed," Rye agreed with a laugh.

"If you really want to give it a go with this woman, to give it an honest shot, you have to remember that it's not all about you."

Rye let out a puff. "Yeah, I know. I've never been terribly good at that."

"That doesn't mean you can't learn. Maybe you're ready. Maybe she's the one. If my life has shown me anything, it's that it's all about the right person at the right time."

"Thanks."

"So, how long have you two been seeing each other?"

"I met her Thursday night."

"You mean three days ago? Man, she must really be something for you to be falling so hard after only a long weekend."

"She is. And I am."

"Daddy, are you coming?" the girls called.

"Go on, man," Rye said. "Put your flamingo swimmies on. I want to watch them take you for a ride."

"Oh, you think it's funny?" Billy joked.

"Actually, I think it's beautiful."

6

As RYE PULLED UP TO THE VALET, HE NOTICED DEE FID-geting. He rubbed her arm, smiled, and said, "Billy and I go way back. We're tight. Other than Oliver, who I've only met briefly, they're all good friends of mine. Don't think of them as famous. You'll be fine."

"It's not that. I told you celebrity doesn't impress me. I'm just a little shy meeting new people."

He took her hand, lifted it to his lips, and kissed it gently. She smiled just as the valets opened their doors. As soon as Rye stepped out in his black slacks, a light black cashmere sweater, and his signature aviator sunglasses, the paparazzi started snapping away. Dee emerged from the car in the black jumpsuit that Troy had insisted she wear. She looked down, trying to avoid the onslaught of flashing lights. He grabbed her hand and they rushed inside. He slipped his sunglasses into a case in his pocket. "Come on, sweetheart. We're meeting them in the bar," he said, leading the way. They immediately spotted William Sumner and his wife Susan sitting close to one another on stools at the glossy mahogany bar. The Sumners wore matching black-and-white outfits, and each sipped sparkling water with muddled mint leaves. Dee noted that he was shorter in person than she'd imagined, just a man whispering sweetly to his ordinary-looking wife, a far cry from the superhero single-handedly saving the world.

"Susan, you look lovely tonight," Rye said, giving her a hug. "Billy, twice in one day. Great to see you, man."

"You too, buddy. Who's your friend?" Billy asked.

"This is Dee Schwartz."

"Very nice to meet you," Billy said, extending his hand.

"Likewise," Dee replied.

"This is my better half, Susan."

Susan smiled brightly, and they said hello to one another. "Dee Schwartz. That sounds familiar. What do you do?" she asked.

Before Dee could respond, Susan's phone started vibrating. She looked at the screen and rolled her eyes dramatically. "Un-freaking-believable. It's him again," she muttered to her husband. "I'm sorry. I need to take this. Please excuse me."

"Don't take any crap! Just breathe, baby," Billy called after her. He turned to Rye and Dee and said, "Don't mind her. She's been dealing with a snarky director and lead actor who are having the proverbial creative differences. Producers get all the headaches. Same bullshit, different day. We did an hour of Transcendental Meditation this morning; hopefully, she can stay centered."

Rye laughed. "Who are you, man? I remember the days when you would snort coke off the navel of some girl you'd just met, and then take a downer to relax."

"Ah, those were the days," Billy joked.

"I'm just kidding," Rye said. "You and Susan never looked better."

"We're doin' alright, doin' alright," he replied with a grin. "The kids are driving us nuts, but in the best way. They kept me in the pool so long today that my skin is still pruned. So, what are you two drinking?"

"Oh, a dirty martini please," Dee said.

Rye draped his arm around her, and she cozied into him. He kissed the side of her head before saying, "Whiskey on the rocks for me."

Billy looked at them for a moment, a soft smile in his eyes, and he signaled to the bartender. Suddenly, the energy in the room shifted as Grey and Sloane Hewson sauntered in. They were impossible to miss, movie star written all over them. Dee watched as everyone in the bar shifted in their seats and casually turned to catch a glimpse of them out of the corners of their eyes. Grey, with his lustrous salt-and-pepper hair and chiseled face, sported a black Armani suit, and Sloane, her dark hair cascading down her petite frame, eyes like almonds, lips stained red, wore a simple nude wrap dress. The embodiment of Hollywood elegance, they took each step as if on an invisible red carpet.

"Billy, Rye, good to see you," Grey said, extending his hand.

"Nice to see you both," Sloane said, pecking each man on the cheek. "We saw Susan outside. Looked like she was giving someone an earful."

"That's my baby," Billy replied proudly.

Rye introduced Dee, and then Grey ordered two glasses of pinot noir. When they all had their drinks in hand, Grey said, "Let's toast."

Before he could continue, in walked Seymour Peretz, the head of Global Pictures, the most successful movie studio in the world. A towering man with shocking white hair in his early seventies, Seymour was unequivocally the most powerful person in Hollywood. All four actors had worked with him, some of them more than once. He had launched Grey's career. He was known for being shrewd, uncompromising, and tight-fisted, but indisputably brilliant.

"This town is so small. Peretz just walked in," Grey informed them quietly. They all turned and smiled politely as Seymour made a beeline over to them.

"Seymour, great to see you," Grey said, flashing his signature smile.

Seymour shook his hand and then turned to Dee with a giant grin. "Dee Schwartz! This is a hell of a surprise," he said, wrapping her in a bear hug.

"So good to see you. It's been too long," she replied as they embraced.

They all watched, dumbfounded. Rye couldn't help staring, a little lost. Billy looked at him curiously and raised an eyebrow. Rye shook his head ever so slightly, signaling his confusion.

When Seymour finally let Dee go, he said, "How's your father enjoying Florida?"

"Still loves it. You should see him—he's like the chief retiree slash party planner in his community. He's corralled a group of guys to play poker and golf, calls them the Brooklyn Eight."

Seymour laughed. "I can picture it. Maybe someday I'll join them, and we can be the Brooklyn Nine. So, what are you doing with this group of scene-stealers?"

"Just dinner. Rye invited me."

Rye put his hand on the small of her back.

"Uh-huh," Seymour grumbled disapprovingly. He looked at Rye and sternly said, "You better treat this one well. She's very special to me, like family. She's a rare gem." Rye looked embarrassed, but before he could respond, Seymour turned to the group and continued, "And she saved one of my biggest pictures."

Dee looked down, blushing. "Really, it was nothing. I just gave you a few notes," she said softly.

"A few notes? You disemboweled it!" Seymour exclaimed, breaking out into hearty laughter. The group was rapt, all listening eagerly. "It was one of those films that was a disaster from day one. Big ideas, lots of talent, but nothing went right. When I saw the rough cut, I almost had a stroke. I asked Dee to give it a look. There was no one else I could trust. I was hoping she'd tell me it wasn't so bad or suggest some minor tweaks, but she tore the sucker to shreds."

"Well, I wouldn't say that."

He snorted. "She eviscerated it, but then she convinced me how we could fix it. We reshot a couple of scenes, which cost us an arm and a leg, and then we recut nearly the whole damn thing. By the end, she had done so much that we offered her a writing credit and a producing credit. She wouldn't take anything, not even a consulting fee."

She looked at him and said, "You've been in Hollyland too long, Seymour. Remember that thing called a favor? It's something some-one does for a friend without expecting anything in return."

He chuckled.

"Besides, I did ask you for something and you gave it to me."

He chuckled again and said, "She asked me to give the public a better piece of art."

"And you did. It's an excellent film. Much better than that pile of shit you started with."

They all burst into laughter, still a bit dumbfounded.

"You're right about that, Dee. I have the Oscars to prove it."

She rolled her eyes. "Awards are ridiculous. But it's a fine film. I was glad to help."

"People say that, but you're the only person I know who means it. Don't ever change. Listen, if you're in town for a while, I could use your help again, and I'd love to catch up."

"I'm a full-time left coaster these days. Sold my loft. It's only been a couple of months. I was planning to call you."

"My own little Dorothy living in Oz. You don't miss Gotham?"

She laughed. "I pop back to New York on occasion. I was actually there a couple of weeks ago for work. I stopped by Friedman's for blintzes and thought of you and Rose."

He smiled. "I'm glad you're here because I'm a few weeks away from the rough edit on a project that's important to me. I think it's going to be a winner, but I'd love your opinion. No heavy lifting, just your honest take. I know you hate driving in LA. I'll send a car to bring you to the studio screening room whenever you're free. Bring friends, Ryder, whoever you want. Will you please watch it for me?"

"Will there be popcorn?"

He laughed. "Natural popcorn with real butter because you're not from LA. I remember."

She giggled. "Then it's a deal. I'd be honored to watch your film."

He squeezed her arms and said, "You're an angel. I'm in New York next week, but I'll be in touch when I get back." He turned to the group. "I'm hoping to have time to catch a show while I'm there. Any recommendations?"

"*Glow* on Broadway is the must-see right now," Sloane said. "Swept the Tonys."

"That's right," Grey agreed. "The other big one is that Greek tragedy they've somehow turned into a musical."

"Susan and I want to see that," Billy interjected.

Dee looked down, biting her lip. Seymour took her hand and said, "You always see everything. What do you suggest?"

"I've seen both those shows and they're very good, but . . ."

"Tell me," Seymour said.

"There's a small production at that tiny Minetta Lane Theatre in the Village. No one you've ever heard of, no sets to speak of, very raw, but it's wonderful. The best of what art can do. I was deeply moved."

"I'll have my assistant get tickets."

"Afterward, you should go to dinner at the Minetta Tavern. Best burgers in the city. And I know you—you'll think that if the burger is good, the steak must be better. Trust me, get the burger."

"I'll do just that. Rose will be sorry to hear she missed you. Come over for dinner one night? And don't forget, when I'm back in town, please come watch my new film. In fact, do it at the end of the day so you can ride home with me for dinner after."

"Sure. Please send Rose my love."

He gave her a long, friendly hug. "I'm late for my reservation. Nice to see you all. Enjoy your evening," he said, walking away.

Noticing everyone staring at her, their mouths agape, Dee explained, "He's an old family friend; we go way back. He and my father grew up together."

"I've worked with Seymour for decades and I've never known him to want anyone's advice about anything, especially his films," Grey said.

"Really? Count yourself lucky then," she replied.

Rye rubbed her back, she looked at him, and he kissed her lightly. "Is Seymour the family friend you told me about? The one who flew you to LA for your school breaks?" he whispered.

"Uh-huh."

"So when you said you went to movie sets, you meant you actually went to active movie sets."

"Yeah."

He smiled and kissed her cheek. "You are just full of surprises."

Susan came bounding in. "Sorry about that. My phone is officially turned off for the night. I saw Oliver waiting for the valet. What did I miss?"

"Oh, not much, just Dee charming the hell out of Seymour Peretz. You should have seen it; he was like putty in her hands," Billy said.

"I'm impressed," Susan said.

"Before Oliver gets here, we never had that toast," Grey pointed out. "To making this happen."

"Cheers!" they all said, clinking glasses.

"Hello, hello, sorry I'm late. The LA traffic never ceases," Oliver said as he shook hands and greeted each member of the group. "My wife sends her regrets. Our youngest wasn't feeling well, so she decided to stay home." He turned his attention to Dee. "You look familiar, but I don't believe we've had the pleasure."

"This is my girlfriend, Dee Schwartz," Rye said.

Dee looked at him, a little surprised. "Good evening, it's nice to meet you," she said to Oliver, extending her hand.

"Likewise. Hmm. You do look awfully familiar," he repeated, studying her face.

"Oliver, what can we get you to drink?" Grey asked.

"Gin and tonic with a piece of lime."

Grey signaled the bartender, who promptly served the cocktail. After making small talk for a few minutes, Grey cut to the chase. "So Oliver, what did you think of the script?"

"It's compelling. Meaty roles for each of you," he replied.

"We fell in love with it," Billy said.

"It's the perfect mix of drama and heart," Rye added.

"You Americans don't waste any time," Oliver said with a laugh. "Straight away to business."

"It is rather boorish of them, isn't it?" Sloane said with an effortlessly charming expression on her face.

They all smiled and chuckled.

Grey jumped back in. "The financing is in place, we're all

producing and starring in it, and the studio is one hundred percent behind this for major distribution. You know that the right director can make or break a film. We want you. You're our guy. What will it take?"

"I'm interested, obviously it's tempting, but I'm quite careful about which projects I tackle these days. I . . ." he trailed off, staring at Dee. "I'm sorry, forgive my staring. I'm just desperately trying to place you. Do you work in the industry?"

"Me? No. I'm an arts researcher and a writer."

He looked at her quizzically for a moment, and then a flash of recognition swept across his face. "Dee Schwartz. Wait, you're not *Deanna Schwartz? Dr. Deanna Schwartz?*"

"Yes," she replied.

"Holy shit," he said, his eyes popping out of his head. "This is an honor, truly. I'm speechless. I've never met an actual legend before." Dee looked down as if searching for a way to respond while the famous movie stars looked on, utterly confused. "You're absolutely brilliant, a genius!" Oliver continued.

"I assure you, I'm not."

"You most certainly are. I'm in awe of your work. I have so many questions to ask you. I could talk to you all night."

Rye looked at her curiously and squeezed her hand.

Oliver turned to the group. "Well, isn't this an unexpected treat? Here I thought it was just going to be another night of Hollywood schmoozing. Shall we head to our table to chat?"

"Uh, sure," Grey stuttered, looking blankly at Billy and Rye, and then at Dee.

"Splendid. Dee, I have so much to discuss with you," Oliver said. Rye motioned for Oliver and Dee to lead the way.

Grey looked at his friends inquisitively, furrowing his brow, and he and Sloane headed to the table.

Billy whispered to Rye, "Seymour Peretz? Oliver Spence? Who the hell is this girl?"

He chuckled. "She's the girl who stole my heart."

7

THEY WALKED INTO THE LARGE DINING ROOM THAT featured wood floors, chocolate-brown leather chairs, and tables draped with white linens—LA's version of an upscale steakhouse. After they were escorted to a large, round table, Rye pulled out Dee's chair, sitting beside her. An empty seat was left between her and Grey. Oliver sat opposite Dee and talked nonstop, unable to take his eyes off her, as if completely starstruck.

"There's no one who's done more to support the arts," Oliver gushed. "My God, your research has forever changed art education and paved the way for arts integration on an international scale, impacting curriculum across the disciplines."

Dee blushed.

"Heavens, I imagine your work has been cited in arts and science research funded in the billions of dollars. Is that so?"

"Uh, well, I'm not really sure. Maybe something like that," Dee said, seemingly embarrassed by the attention. Rye took her hand under the table, massaging her fingers.

"I've heard that it's standing room only at your lectures around the world. In scholarly circles, you're a rock star, an icon."

"I've never been comfortable with the attention. Thank goodness it doesn't translate to the rest of the world. The work is all that matters," she replied. "Everything else is a distraction. Besides, what I've been able to do so far has just been a drop in the bucket. There's a long road ahead that many are traveling."

Oliver smiled. "Your *Brains on Art* books fundamentally changed how people understand art and science. I've read every word. I have about a million questions. What on earth is it like to be the only person to understand something so deeply?"

"I assure you, that's not the case."

"But it is! Weren't you something like thirty years old when you started winning lifetime achievement awards? Well deserved of course, but what must that have felt like?"

Rye looked at her, surprise and adoration swirling in his eyes.

As if too excited to wait for a response, Oliver continued, "And of course you're a talented artist in your own right. Your writing is sublime, the poetry and novellas. Beautifully unapologetic. Fearless. Real art."

"Thank you," Dee said.

"That's how I know you!" Susan exclaimed. "My production company looked into optioning the entertainment rights to one of your books a couple of years ago. As I recall, we were told you weren't interested. That was a first."

"Please don't be offended. It's just not for me."

"Well, maybe I can change your mind," Susan replied.

"She can be quite persuasive," Billy said.

"Wait a minute, I know your creative writing," Sloane said. "Oliver's right. You're enormously talented. Your work is, um, how shall I say it? Audacious. Irreverent. The reviewers have branded you a female Bukowski. Don't you find that maddening? It's so misogynist."

Dee smiled. "I'm sure you know better than most what critics are like. They love to create false comparisons. They have no idea what to make of a woman's work on its own. Luckily, I'm not interested in what they think. I make art simply because it brings me joy. There's no other reason."

Sloane smiled faintly and the table fell silent, as if they were all contemplating what those words meant in their own lives.

"Honestly, I was just looking for a creative means of uncensored expression. I didn't consider what anyone would think. The reason I started writing poetry and novellas instead of some other, more popular forms was because hardly anyone reads them," Dee explained.

"Yet your poetry collections and works of fiction have all become best sellers. Seems as though people do read them, critics too," Oliver said.

"Yeah, it was a flawed plan."

Rye laughed.

A waiter came over, but before he could say a word, Grey put his hand up and said, "We'd like to relax for a little while before we order. I think we're all set with drinks for now. Thank you." The waiter nodded and walked off. Grey continued, refocusing the conversation on the task at hand. "Oliver, we'd love to hear your vision for the film. Maybe we can bat around ideas and see where it gets us. We all feel strongly that you're the right person, the *only* person, for the job."

"Absolutely," Billy said.

"You're our guy," Rye added.

Oliver took a sip of his drink and looked directly at Dee. "Did Ryder tell you about the film?"

Dee looked around the table, visibly uneasy that all eyes were upon her again. Grey smiled at her, flashing his dimples, encouraging her to respond.

"Uh, yes, he told me a little about it."

"You know more about art than anyone at this table, hell, than anyone in the world as far as I can tell, and you understand the importance of making good art. I respect your opinion enormously. What do you think? Is it a worthwhile project?" Oliver asked.

Before she could respond, Dazz, one of the most successful hip-hop artists in the world, approached their table with another man in tow. Grey and Sloane noticed and immediately rose to greet him.

"Dazz, it's great to see you," Grey said, shaking his hand. "LA gets smaller by the minute. It's a veritable who's who here tonight. I think the last time I saw you was backstage at the Golden Globes."

"Wonderful to see you," Sloane added, pecking Dazz on the cheek.

"Likewise. Chris and I were in the studio down the block, trying to wrap up my new record. We've been holed up for weeks. We got sick of getting takeout brought in, so we wandered over for a proper meal. Please, sit. I don't want to interrupt your night."

Grey and Sloane took their seats. "Have you met everyone?" Grey asked, prepared to make introductions.

Dazz turned to greet the others. His mouth fell open when he noticed Dee. "I don't believe it. This is a gift from God. *The professor is in the house!*" he bellowed gleefully. Dee jumped up and they embraced.

"So good to see you," she said. "Have you met Rye, Billy, Susan, and Oliver?" she asked.

They all said hello, Rye looking at her curiously yet again.

"Dee, this is a sign. Can we talk?" Dazz turned to the table and said, "Would you mind if we joined you for a minute?"

"Of course not," Sloane said as they all welcomed them.

"The more the merrier," Billy added, shooting Rye a mischievous look.

Grey signaled to the waiter to bring another chair. Chris pulled back the empty chair beside Dee and sat down, and Dazz squeezed a chair in next to him. He turned to Dee and said, "We need to put my new record to bed. The lead single is keeping me up at night. We've been working on it for days, but we're just spinning our wheels. Brought in half a dozen producers. Everyone thinks I'm being obsessive and that it's good to go . . ."

"Because it is," Chris interrupted.

Dazz shook his head. "It's not there yet. Can't put my finger on it, but it's missing something. This isn't a coincidence; seeing you here is a blessing."

Chris made a sour face. "We've had the best in the business working on this around the clock. How is she the answer to our prayers?" He turned to Dee. "You in the music business?"

"Uh, no, I'm not. I've actually always suspected I'm slightly tone-deaf."

Chris shook his head incredulously.

"And it gets worse. As Dazz knows, I don't much care for hip-hop," she added. "But don't worry, the genre is just like an outfit. It has nothing to do with the bones of a song."

Rye smiled.

Chris turned to Dazz and said, "We've been hammering this one for damn near a week. Now this tone-deaf white chick is going to have all the answers? You gone crazy?"

"Shut your mouth and show some respect for the professor," Dazz said. He redirected his attention to Dee. "Don't pay attention to him. He doesn't understand your genius."

"Oh, I like him. He's refreshingly honest," she replied.

"Please, help me out and do your three-listen thing," Dazz said.

"Well, I'd be happy to listen to it, but this really isn't a good time," she said, glancing around the table.

"They're artists; they understand. The song is only three minutes and thirty-five seconds long. It'll take you ten minutes, fifteen tops." Dazz turned to the group. "You don't mind, do you? The song has a strong social justice message meant to uplift and empower the disenfranchised. It's supposed to be an anthem people can dance to, so it needs to be perfect."

Never one to miss the chance to publicly support a good cause, Sloane squeezed Grey's bicep. "You know Grey and I are always happy to do all we can to promote equality."

"Yes, of course," Grey added. "The night is young. By all means, Dee, don't let us stop you."

Dee bit her lip and turned to Rye. He put his hand on her thigh and smiled warmly. She looked at Dazz and said, "Let me hear it once, so I know what the deal is. We'll take it from there, okay?"

"You're a godsend. Chris, give it to her."

Chris rolled his eyes but opened his backpack and took out an MP3 player and large headphones.

"Please lower the volume a bit. I know how loud this one listens to music, and I don't want to blow my eardrums out," Dee said.

Dazz laughed. Chris adjusted the volume and handed it to her. "Just push that button when you're ready."

"Thank you," she replied. "Please excuse me for a moment," she said to the group as she put on the headphones. She hit play and closed her eyes. A few seconds later, a smile washed across her face.

Dazz watched her intently. "Dude, she likes it. She's smiling," he said quietly to Chris.

Chris furrowed his brow and shrugged.

"Dude, just pay attention. I'm telling you, in fifteen minutes you'll be asking me what the hell just happened. You'll be replaying this moment in your mind for the rest of your life. This chick is seriously plugged into something. Reggie Harris said he's never seen anyone who can do what she does."

"Reggie Harris? As in the Godfather of Soul, creator of the most important Black record label of all time? He don't like white people." Everyone at the table tried to muffle their laughter. Chris noticed and said, "No offense."

"None taken," Rye said, taking a swig of his drink.

Continuing in a hushed tone so as not to interrupt Dee, not caring that the others were all listening in, Dazz said, "Brother, that doesn't apply to her. When she's in the room, no one else is there. Reggie once told me the only other people who could do what she does were Harry and Ray, the ultimate legends. And she can do it with any kind of art, not just music."

"Seriously?"

"You know Green, the anonymous street artist?"

Chris nodded.

"We were having dinner with him once . . ."

"Wait, you know his real identity?" Chris asked.

"She introduced us. They're tight. We were sitting at the bar, and he said he wanted to do a big experiential type of installation. Dude, she took a cocktail napkin, sketched out the whole thing. Brother, it took her three minutes. We hadn't even been served our drinks. He added a title and some details during dinner. Six months later, it became the most famous piece of art of its kind. Millions of people from around the world flocked to it."

Billy and Grey looked at Rye. He shook his head in disbelief and looked at Dee, who was still lost in the music, her eyes shut.

Chris's eyes were like saucers. He paused to watch her for a moment, bopping her head silently to the beat of the music in her ears. "Well, if she's the key to getting the song right, why don't you just pay her whatever it takes?"

Dazz shook his head. "Her time isn't for sale. Not to anyone, not for any price. She has to *want* to do it, like a favor. And bro, if she's willing to teach you, you better listen and learn. She's taught me a bunch of stuff, but it's easier to apply to producing other people's work. With this one, I'm too close." Dazz noticed Dee taking the headphones off, and he looked at her expectantly.

"Dazz!" she said, smiling brightly. "*Those lyrics.*"

"You like 'em?"

"White people will be terrified. They're perfect!"

Everyone laughed.

"It's super catchy, not at all what I expected. It's like trap music taken to a new place. So clever to start with the chorus, then go into the verse and then the pre-chorus. And those three drops, damn. Well done. I'm impressed."

"It's great, isn't it?" Chris asked.

"It's very good."

"Well, how good is it? What would you rate it on a scale of one to ten?" Chris asked.

"That's subjective," she replied. She turned toward Dazz. "Damn, this must be killing you. It's so close to greatness, and I know what a perfectionist you are."

"I knew you'd hear it," Dazz said.

"Look, I'm in, but obviously this isn't a good time."

"We have to put this thing to bed; we've already missed our deadline. Please, do your thing. Just two more listens."

"Dazz, that's a bare minimum. It doesn't always work. Sometimes it takes hours or days, still with no guarantee that I could be of any use. I can't promise you anything more than what I've already said."

"I'm cool with that."

She looked around the table, all eyes upon her. She lowered her voice and said, "Dazz, I'm just a guest at this dinner. Oliver Spence is here for a business meeting, and . . ."

"Oh, please," Oliver interjected. "This is truly a thrill. It's making my evening, my year! I know what you're going to do, and I'd be elated to bear witness. I can't believe my good fortune. I'm sure everyone feels that way."

Everyone looked at Oliver, and then at Dee. "Absolutely," Grey said.

"Please, we're fascinated," Billy added.

Rye brushed his fingers against her thigh and nodded softly, smiling his encouragement. She looked down, shook her head, and mumbled, "Fuck." Then, with laser focus on Dazz, she said, "Yeah, okay. But we're gonna have to do this old school."

"What do you need?" Dazz asked.

"A copy of the lyrics, something to write with, a glass of ice, and if they could make it five degrees cooler in here, that would be great. Then I need you to make sure no one comes to the table until we're done. If I'm interrupted, there really isn't time to start again." She turned to Chris and asked, "You know the song?"

"Yes," he said, looking at her with a new reverence.

"Good, you can help."

"Whatever you need."

"On the second listen, I want you to tap out the beat on my leg. I need to count three things at once, which is difficult under the best of circumstances, and these are *not* the best of circumstances," she said, looking around the crowded restaurant.

"You got it." Chris handed her the lyrics and a pen while Dazz spoke with the waiter, who returned a moment later with a glass of ice before scurrying away.

"Dee, why don't you explain to everyone what you're going to do," Oliver suggested, grinning like a schoolboy about to have a magic trick revealed. "It really is mind-blowing. I'm sure Chris would be eager to learn."

"Please," Chris said, looking at her wide-eyed.

"We're all interested," Billy said, putting his arm around Susan and settling in for the show.

"I'm certainly intrigued," Rye said quietly, taking her hand under the table.

Dee smiled. "Okay. Well, every piece of art has artistic and scientific components. The more closely aligned these aspects are, the stronger the piece of art. When something isn't working and you can't figure out why, you need to separate the art from the science, the content from the form, look at them on their own and then put them back together."

"Science?" Chris asked.

"Yeah. Neuroscience, physics, math. It's the most obvious with music because of the timing, which is a mathematical system, but it's true for a painting, a novel, a film, whatever. Here," she said, grabbing the saltshaker off the table. "If I unscrew this top, you can clearly see how the salt can be separated from the shaker, right?"

They all nodded.

"Think of the container as the science and the salt as the art." She paused and sprinkled some salt on her bread plate. She picked up a single grain and put it in the palm of her hand. "Of course, it's more complicated with art because the form and content, or the art and science, aren't put together artificially. They come into existence as a unified whole. They're melded together, like this grain of salt. The grain is the delivery system; it's the form in which we experience the salt. It's the science. But the *flavor*, which is what we really care about, that's the essence of the salt. It's the art. What Dazz wants me to do is extract the flavor from the grain."

Oliver smiled brightly. "It's brilliant, absolutely brilliant."

Dee blushed.

"How are you going to do that?" Chris asked.

"First, I'll listen to just the art—how it moves me as a listener, how it makes me feel physically and emotionally. Then, I'll analyze the science, the structure and timing."

"What's the ice for?" Chris asked, totally enthralled.

"Since we don't have the benefit of gadgets in the studio, I'm going to have to use my own pulse to count. My heart rate will go up after the first listen, and I'll need to slow it back down. Ice is a quick fix. Or we could all go outside and smoke some peyote."

They all laughed. Chris looked at her, wanting to be respectful but not sure whether to take her seriously.

"I'm just kidding," she said. "Actually, it's better to learn to use your own pulse; that way you never need anything except what you already possess. We're all built with the most reliable clock in the world right inside of us. I can do it regardless of my heart rate, but it's easier to count multiple things when it's slower, and given these surroundings," she said, again looking around the boisterous restaurant, "I'll take whatever break I can."

She retrieved her cell phone from her handbag and placed it on the table beside the lyrics. She spent a minute studying the lyric sheet and then said, "It would be helpful if no one spoke until we're done." Everyone nodded in agreement. She turned to Chris and said, "After the first listen, I'll stop to take notes and slow my heart rate. No matter what I do, please don't speak to me and break my concentration."

"What are you going to do?" Chris asked.

"Did you ever see the deli scene in *When Harry Met Sally*?"

He nodded apprehensively.

"This won't be that bad, but I need to be free. I need to tune everyone and everything out, which admittedly is a little challenging with this group," she said, glancing around the table of celebrities.

They all chuckled.

"Chris, when I'm ready, I'll put your hand on my leg and nod, and then you keep the beat; do it hard and please don't stop until I tell you to."

He nodded.

"Dazz, any constraints on the length?"

"No. It's well under the standard four minutes for radio, so a little longer or shorter won't matter."

"Okay." She put the headphones on, closed her eyes, and hit play a moment later. Everyone watched as she started moving her head in time and throwing one of her hands out, methodically gesturing with her fingers. As the song progressed, her movements quickened. By the end, she was nearly jumping out of her seat, her hair whipping around. Without looking at anyone, she took the headphones off, stuck an ice cube in her mouth, and scribbled notes on the lyric sheet, underlining and circling words. Then, with her head down, she took another ice cube and rubbed it on her wrists. A minute later, she took several slow, considered breaths, and then took her pulse. Everyone's eyes remained glued to her. She put the headphones back on, set the stopwatch on her phone, placed Chris's hand on her leg, and nodded at him. He began tapping out the beat. She placed two fingers on her neck and hit play again. She picked up her pen and began making numbered notations throughout the lyric sheet. When the song was over, she took the headphones off and gestured at Chris to stop. She looked at the lyric sheet again and made additional notations. She used the calculator on her phone to check some numbers. She turned her gaze to Dazz, smiled brightly, and announced, "I've got it."

"Tell me," he begged.

"I heard it on the first listen and then again on the second, but I couldn't figure out why *you* couldn't hear it, so I didn't trust myself. It wasn't until the last listen that I got it. The final drop leading into the chorus is the emotional center of the song. That's when you bring it home, but you're not going far enough. Right now, it mimics the two proceeding drops, but it needs to be longer. It needs four more beats."

Dazz looked at her, a sunny smile sweeping across his face. He glanced at Chris, whose eyes sparkled with amazement.

Dee continued, "Chris, you asked me how good the song is. Well, the third drop is the climax, and in this current version, he's blowing his wad too early. There's no pow. How good do you think sex is without an orgasm? Right now, that's how good the song is—still fun but ultimately unsatisfying."

Everyone tried to muffle their laughter. Rye was hysterical, his face red.

Dee continued undaunted, "Listen to it in your mind from the second drop to the end. You'll see."

Both men shut their eyes. A minute later, Dazz said, "Unbelievable."

Everyone at the table looked at one another in awe. Rye couldn't close his mouth, his smile was so wide.

"Dee," Chris said, "I hear it, but if we add four beats, won't it throw off the whole structure of the song?"

"I think everyone from Wynton Marsalis to Queen would insist that you can build any structure you want, but I don't disagree with your instinct given your genre. There are other ways to create balance, and I know Dazz always wants the numbers to line up. Here, I've given you three options," she explained, showing them the marked-up lyric sheet. "Any of these will be better than what you have, and you'll create perfect symmetry. None of them changes the overall time by more than sixteen seconds. This option," she said, pointing, "doesn't change the overall time at all, and I think it's your winner. Try them all in the studio. I'm sure you'll come up with additional options too."

"How did we miss this?" Chris asked.

"Because you betrayed the art to make the math work. If the art and the science can be perfectly aligned, great. That's not always possible, and when it's not, you should never sacrifice the art for the science. The art is always what matters. At the end of the day, audiences will forgive an imperfect song with moving lyrics," she said, glancing at Rye, "or a film with an imperfect plot but characters they care about, which is why what they do is so important," she said, gesturing to the actors at the table. Rye smiled and took her hand. "Dazz has an incredible internal clock. His natural inclination is always to make the math work. He's gifted in that way. Unlike most of us, he's able to do it without even thinking about it. That's why he couldn't hear it even though he knew something wasn't quite right." She paused for a moment. "You see, sometimes it's just the question we're asking. I knew where the trouble spot was on the first listen, but then I had to ask myself why Dazz didn't hear it. It's like with Oliver tonight," she said, glimpsing across the table. "He knows there are no guarantees when making art, but he wants to spend his time on quality projects. He's sitting over there wondering whether he wants to work with three make-believe superheroes. Perhaps the question he should be asking instead is whether he wants to work with three *real* superheroes. What Rye, Billy, and Grey have achieved in cinema is nothing short of astonishing. They're a dream team."

Oliver looked around the table until his gaze landed back on Dee. He nodded his head in agreement.

Dee continued to speak directly to Chris. "Over the course of this evening, both Oliver and Dazz have called me a genius. I'm not.

But I do know that Oliver has a rare chance to make a piece of art that has an extraordinary probability of being something truly special, *and* I know that Dazz's song needs four more beats."

Rye squeezed Dee's hand, and then he, Billy, and Grey exchanged the subtlest of smiles.

"Dee, will you teach it to me? What you did?" Chris asked earnestly.

"Sure. I'll give you some homework. Once you've mastered it, ask Dazz how to get in touch with me. Did you ever see *The Karate Kid*?"

He nodded.

"This is my version of 'wax on, wax off.' Think of it as circle, square." Chris listened intently as she continued, "Envision a bright white circle in your mind, and absolutely nothing else. Hold the vision for a full five minutes without allowing any other thought to enter your mind for even a second. Once you're able to do that, picture a circle and a square, side by side. Hold the vision for five minutes without any other interruptions. Finally, envision the circle and square. Watch them move until they are on top of each other. Hold that single thought for five minutes."

"You can do that?" he asked.

She smiled. "I'm doing it right now."

"Damn, you are a badass, huh? Okay, I'll work on it. Thank you," Chris said.

"It'll take you a while, and it'll be frustrating, but once you can do it, call me. Just remember: circle, square."

Dazz signaled to the waiter, who was standing by. "Please bring my friends three bottles of Cristal, three bottles of sparkling water, a vegetarian mezze platter, a cheese and charcuterie board, and Beluga with blinis. Keep it coming and then put their whole bill on my tab."

"Very good, sir," the waiter said, darting off.

"That's very generous. Thank you," Grey said.

"Yes, thank you," they all echoed.

"I apologize for holding up your dinner. Please excuse our interruption," Dazz said sincerely. He stood up and turned to Dee. "Can I at least thank you in the liner notes?"

"Don't even think about it," she said, rising to hug him.

"I hope I didn't ruin your evening."

"I'll let you know," she replied, glancing back at Rye with a wink.

Dazz smiled, hugged her again, and waved goodbye to everyone. He and Chris left without ever having gotten the food they came in for. Dee sat down and Rye draped his arm around her, squeezing her shoulder. She looked intently into his blue eyes. Waiters came rushing over, popped bottles of champagne and sparkling water, and placed a flute in front of each guest. When their glasses were full, Oliver raised his and said, "I would like to propose a toast: to our new film project. I'm in!"

Rye, Billy, and Grey smiled widely and practically leapt out of their seats in surprise. Susan rubbed Billy's shoulder, and Sloane exchanged a congratulatory look with her husband.

"Cheers!" everyone exclaimed.

Dee took a sip of her champagne as Rye leaned over and kissed her cheek.

"I got up and tried to mask my embarrassment, but I was like, 'Yeah, okay, the stunt guy can do this one!'" Rye said.

They all laughed hysterically. The waiter came by to refill their tea and coffee cups. Oliver placed his hand over his cup and shook his head. He turned to Dee, who had been quiet as the men exuberantly traded stories during their lavish, three-course meal.

"Dee, I fear the evening is ending soon and there's still so much I want to ask you."

"Oh, I don't want to bore everyone," she said. "I think these guys are much more fun."

"Nonsense. Just tell me this: What inspired you to study the arts in the unique way you have? What do you want next?"

"I love the arts, have since I was a little girl. Sitting in a movie theater, going to a concert, reading a novel, it all just seemed magical. Who wouldn't benefit from more magic in their lives?" Rye put his arm around her, and she nuzzled closer to him. "At some point, I realized that for all the arts bring to our lives, they aren't valued. Our education system is proof of that. I had the foolish idea that if I could explain the science of art, explore how people experience art and learn from it, that maybe we'd start to value it more." She stopped and sighed. "But truthfully, it's all bullshit."

Oliver looked stunned. "Why do you say that?"

"Don't misunderstand me. Everything I've researched and written is true; it's just that it shouldn't matter. We should value art for art's sake. But sometimes people can't see what's right in front of them, so you have to give them a way to see it."

Oliver smirked and said, "You're like the Wizard of Oz, the woman behind the curtain, showing everyone the gold dust they already possess, their power."

She smiled. "Funny, my friend Seymour has always called me his Dorothy. Perhaps the yellow brick road was really just a trail of gold dust connecting one dream to another."

Rye hung on every word, his eyes fixed on Dee.

"You've done enormous good. Your work has changed education and research the world over," Oliver said.

She sighed. "There's been a personal price to pay. In my effort to give more people access to the magic of the arts, I've lost it myself in some ways." She paused, looked around the table, and said, "I love and see value in all art. Children's art, street art, doodles in someone's scrapbook, novice actors on community theater stages. I find beauty in it all. Some of my favorite artists are people you've never heard of. There's so much unrecognized talent. There's no place in my heart that wants to critique art—quite the opposite, in fact. But somehow along the way, people have taken my work and turned me into some kind of art oracle, like my friend Seymour or like Dazz tonight. He didn't want me to listen to his new song for pleasure or out of a desire to share his art, but for critical analysis. It's the furthest thing from what I want." She sighed and said, "As for what I want next, I'm just looking for a little of that gold dust you mentioned. I want someone to stroll around a museum with me, someone to take me to a concert or film and ask me, 'Did you enjoy it?' and when I say, 'Yes,' they smile and we move on."

Oliver smiled. The conversation moved on. Dee leaned over and whispered to Rye, "I'm going to step outside for a minute to get some air."

A few minutes later, Dee was leaning against the exterior of the building, her head down. She was taking deep breaths of the night air, trying to steady her nerves. She felt a hand on her back and looked up to see Rye. "Hey," she whispered as their eyes locked. He gently brushed the hair away from her face and ran his fingers along her cheek.

"I'm so sorry about tonight. It was an impossible situation to navigate. I did what I could to redirect the focus. At least it worked out."

"You were spectacular, and I've fallen in love with you."

"What?" she asked, her eyes wide.

"I wanted to say it this morning, but I was gun-shy. Dee, I've never met anyone like you. I don't even know how to describe the way I feel when I'm with you. You are what I've been looking for without even knowing it. I love you. I'm completely in love with you."

"I love you too," she said confidently.

He cupped her face in his hands and kissed her tenderly. Suddenly, they heard a frenzy of flashbulbs. They turned to look, blinded as the paparazzi, snapping away, began yelling, "Ryder, is that your new girlfriend?"

Part Two

8

"Good morning, sweetheart," Rye said, wrapping his arms around Dee.

"Is it morning? We barely slept," she mumbled while yawning.

"I just couldn't get enough of you," he said.

"Me too."

He gently ran his fingertips along her cheek. "Dee, I love you so much. With all my heart."

"I love you too."

"I never expected this, and now it's all that I want. Baby, I've made mistakes in my life, especially with women. With you, I want to get it right."

She smiled and ran her fingers through his hair. "This is so special. You're the most romantic man."

"You bring it out of me." He paused, staring adoringly at her, and said, "I can't stop thinking about dinner. I knew you were smart and talented, but until last night, I didn't realize the depth of your brilliance."

"Rye . . ." she started, looking away, embarrassed by the attention.

"I mean it," he said, touching her chin and bringing her gaze back to meet his. "The things Oliver said, what I witnessed myself— I'm completely in awe. Like Dazz said, you're seriously plugged into something. You're exceptional." He brushed her hair back and continued, "Those *Brains on Art* books of yours that Oliver mentioned are on the top of my reading list. Tell me everything about your research."

She stretched her arms and yawned again.

Rye chuckled and said, "Okay, point taken. You don't have to tell me right now, but I need you to know how impressive what you do is to me. I want to be a part of it, for us to share our passions."

She smiled. "This is what I always wanted."

He kissed her forehead and said, "I'll get dressed and go make us some coffee. Meet me downstairs when you're ready."

"Thank you, honey."

He paused on his way out the door and turned back to look at her and smile.

"What?" she asked.

"Nothing. I just feel like we've been together forever."

"Me too. I've never felt about anyone the way I feel about you. Rye, I want to learn everything about you, and for the first time, I want to share everything about me."

"Me too, sweetheart." He kissed her forehead again and said, "I'll go make that coffee."

After showering and brushing her teeth, Dee wandered down to the kitchen, following the smell of French roast.

"Here you go," Rye said, handing her a mug.

"Thank you," she said, taking a big sip.

"Do you want something to eat?" he asked.

"No, thank you. I'm not hungry. I think I'm just going to enjoy my coffee and catch up on my messages," she replied, plopping down at the table and retrieving her cell phone. "Gee, my phone's really blowing up."

"Everything okay?"

"Uh . . . it seems that trashy website, *Celebs in the Wild*, ran video and photos of us last night outside the restaurant."

Rye sighed. "I usually try to be discreet in public and fly under the radar. I'm sorry. I shouldn't have let that happen."

"It's not your fault. Yikes, I have a voice mail from my dad. Not exactly how I wanted him to find out about us."

"Your dad follows *Celebs in the Wild*?"

"No, of course not. He has my name in his Google alerts. Honestly, it's mostly because he's always trying to catch people plagiarizing my work. It's kind of funny."

"I can give you some privacy if you want to call him."

"No, honey, it's not like that. There's nothing I would say to him that I can't say in front of you." She took a deep breath and dialed her father's number. Rye sat beside her, his hand on her back.

"Hi, Daddy. How are you? . . . Yeah, I've seen it. I'm sorry you heard that way. I was planning to tell you next time we spoke . . . Not that long . . . Dad, it *is* serious. You'll like him, I promise. He's a wonderful man. We have something special . . ." she said, glancing at Rye, who smiled and rubbed her back. "Don't you always say that we should never judge a book by its cover? . . . Yes, I've heard it was a great show. Honestly, I've never seen it . . . Go back to your game; we can chat later . . . Oh, I bumped into Seymour last night . . . Yeah, he and Rose invited me over for dinner . . . Okay. Love you, Daddy. Bye."

"He wasn't happy, huh?" Rye asked.

"He was just surprised, that's all. He'll adjust. He's always skeptical of new people in my life."

"Sounds like he already has an impression of me. I'm used to that."

"I'm sorry. Honey, he'll get to know you and he'll adore you. If it's any consolation, he loved you on *The Mission*."

Rye chuckled. "I'll take what I can get."

"I'm visiting him in about a month. I'm giving a few lectures at schools in New York. I had planned to stop in Florida on the way and spend a couple of days with him. If your schedule allows it, come with me. It would mean so much to me if you met each other; I really think you two will get along famously. Besides, I'd love to have some time in New York with you. It would be magical."

"I would love that. Now that Oliver's on board, we'll start shooting in six weeks, so I should be free to go with you." He leaned forward and kissed her lightly. "What should we do today?"

"Rye, since filming doesn't start for a while, why don't you use this time to work on your music? Finish those songs, get in a studio, hire musicians, and record some of it. Didn't you say you know a producer?"

"Porter Lewis is an old friend of mine."

"Wow, he's great. Everyone in the industry respects him. Doesn't he also co-own a record label?"

Rye smiled. "You really know your stuff. Yeah, and it's pretty successful for an independent label. Not a lot of people know this, but he's also a talented musician in his own right. He can play just about every instrument."

"Well, why not give him a call? I'm sure he could pull together a group of backing musicians." She paused and took his hand. "Even if you decide not to put it out there in the end, why not at least see what you have? You're so passionate about it. Your eyes light up when you talk about it, and you look so free when you're playing."

He kissed her again and whispered, "I love you, Dee. Okay, I'll give it a try. You can work from here, right?"

She nodded. "I just need to swing by my place to pick up my laptop and a few things."

"Good. I want you to stay here with me, by my side while I do this."

"There's nowhere else I want to be."

9

"Rye, let's try it again from the second verse," Porter called. In his early sixties, the lanky, tattooed man ran his studio with the same ease as his subtle Southern drawl.

After spending a week holed up at home with Dee, selecting songs, Rye was two weeks into recording his first album, titled simply, "Ryder Field Unplugged." As she had in the days prior, Dee sat in the back of the room, observing and quietly working on her poetry collection.

"One more time, all the way through," Porter said.

When they finished laying the track, they all huddled together to listen, Rye's arm slung around Dee's waist. After the song ended, Dee leaned over and whispered in his ear. He smiled and said, "Porter, let's hear it without the backing vocals on the chorus."

"We can try that," he replied. He made some adjustments and played the song again. "Yeah, that's good. I like it," Porter said.

"It's better," Rye said. "Cleaner. Fits with the simplicity we're trying to achieve." He kissed Dee on the cheek. "Thank you."

She smiled. "I'm going to get back to my poetry, but I'll be listening."

He kissed her softly and squeezed her hand.

A few hours later, Porter said, "That's it. We have everything for the album recorded. Now it's just a matter of final mixing."

"Actually, I wrote a new song that I'd like to try out. I'm thinking it could be the album closer," Rye said. "This one is solo, just me and the guitar." He turned to the band. "Thanks, guys. We're all set."

As the musicians filed out of the studio, Porter said, "Alright, let's give your new song a listen."

"Dee," Rye called, "would you come up front, sweetheart?"

She put her notebook down and walked over to the monitor.

"I wanted to get you a special gift to show what you mean to me, but nothing seemed like it was enough. I know you don't care about material things. You love art more than anything, so I wrote you a song," Rye said.

Her eyes were wide with surprise.

"Dee, you inspire me, in art and life. This is called, 'Extraordinary,' and it's for you, my love."

Her face lit up. As he began playing the sweet love song with the lines, "I'll be your muse, you'll be mine, my one and only, my extraordinary love," her eyes brimmed with tears. When he finished the song, he put his guitar down and walked over to her.

She sniffled and whispered, "That was so beautiful and romantic. It gave me goose bumps. I don't know what to say. It's the most wonderful present I've ever received."

He wiped her tears away and said, "I always want you to know, in my words and my voice, what you mean to me. You're my greatest love."

"And you're mine."

Later that night when they were crawling into bed, Dee said, "I can't stop thinking about that gorgeous song. I can't believe you wrote that for me. To have inspired such beautiful art . . . Well, I can't tell you what it means to me. When you were playing it, everything else fell away and I felt like there was gold dust floating in the air."

He kissed her. "It just flowed right out of me. You've awoken something in me, something creative and powerful." He rubbed the tip of his nose to the tip of hers. "Thank you for coming to the studio again."

"You don't have to thank me. It's inspiring. I've loved every minute of it," she replied. "I hope Porter didn't mind."

"Not at all. He thinks you have incredible instincts." He smiled and added, "He sees what we have, and he's so happy for me. Truthfully, I think he's a bit jealous, asked me if you had any friends as amazing as you are."

She laughed.

He nuzzled his nose into her neck. "It's so sweet the way you whisper in my ear in the studio when there's something you like or something you think we should try."

She smiled. "I just don't want to get in the way or steal the spotlight."

"You couldn't. I value your opinion more than I can say," he replied, and he kissed her softly. "None of this would be happening without you."

"That's not true. Maybe it would have taken you a little longer to decide to do it, but music is such a big part of who you are. I'm sure you would have done it eventually. You're truly talented."

"Thank you, baby. I still can't believe the record is basically done. It's crazy how fast this has all come together."

"Well, you had a stockpile of great songs, and the musicians Porter found are awesome. It was like you've been playing together for years. It feels like it was all meant to be. You should be proud of what you've created. It's a beautiful, authentic album. It's entirely true to who you are, and I admire that. Deeply."

"That means a lot to me." He paused and ran his hand through his hair pensively. "Listen, I've been talking with my management team, and they think we should drop the album shortly after my movie shoot wraps. It's the only way to make it work before I start shooting the new TV series. I'll have a little time to do press to promote the album, and they can even schedule a short tour of Europe and North America. We're thinking two or three months. I wanted to discuss it with you. If you don't want me to go . . ."

"Rye, I would never stand in your way. I hope you know that by now."

He took both of her hands and said, "Sweetheart, what we have is so special, and I don't want to jeopardize it. To be honest, I've never given up anything in my career before for anyone. But you are different; this relationship is different. It's not just about me any-more. It's about *us*. You are more important to me than the album, more important than any movie or show, too important to take for granted."

"I love you," she said.

He smiled. "I know you've already agreed to go to Montana with me for the film shoot, and I don't want to keep imposing or making you upend your life."

"You're not," she said softly. "I just want to be with you. Being in the mountains will be so inspiring for my writing, and not everyone gets to visit the set of an Oliver Spence film. I'm really excited about it. I can't wait to watch you work."

He fell silent, trying to find the courage to speak again. "When we book the album tour, would you consider coming on the road with me?"

"Really?" she asked, her eyes wide.

"Yes. I've thought a lot about this. I know it's a lot to ask, and I don't even know if it's possible without harming your career, which I would never want to do, but . . ."

"Of course I'll go with you! When you schedule your tour dates, I could book a series of university lectures to coincide with some of your gigs. We'll travel together, see the sights, and I can write. I'll go to work while you're doing sound checks or whatever, and afterward I'll meet you at your shows."

"Come here," he said, and he threw his arms around her and showered her with kisses. She burrowed into him. "You have no idea how much this means to me, how much you mean to me, and what we have together."

"Yes, I do, because I feel the same way," she replied.

"When we get in bed at night and read the scripts I've been sent or the poems you're working on, well . . ."

"What?" she asked, looking up into his eyes.

"Dee, I never knew it could be like this. The way we support each other, the quiet time we have—it's something I look forward to every day."

"Me too."

"Sweetheart, you should be prepared for how hectic the next six months will be. When we get back from Florida and New York, we'll only have a few days before we head to Montana. Then I'll probably take a few weeks off, and then the tour, followed by press junkets for the movie release. Things will finally calm down a bit when I start the new TV series."

"It's been years since you did TV. Are you excited?" she asked.

He kissed the top of her head and said, "After *The Mission*, I needed a break. Plus, none of the scripts that crossed my desk seemed worth that kind of daily grind. But I loved this script, and when it got the Dee Schwartz seal of approval, I knew it was the one. The timing is perfect. Since we're shooting here in LA, I'll have a predict-able schedule, which feels important now that I have you. Life will be more stable."

"Honey, we can live our lives any way we choose."

He tipped her chin up to raise her gaze to meet his. "Sweetheart, I choose you."

10

"THE SALSA FRESCA IS READY," DEE ANNOUNCED.

"Looks great, a hell of a lot better than the jarred version I use," Rye replied as he stirred the refried beans. "Which plates should I grab?"

Dee opened a cabinet and took out a stack of six plates. "Here you go," she said, placing them on the counter.

"When everyone gets here, we can have a drink. Then all I have to do is heat up the tortillas and cook the eggs, you can slice up some avocados, and we should be good to go."

"Thank you for coming to my place to do this."

"It's my pleasure," he replied.

"I feel badly because I've been so blissfully preoccupied with you that I've missed my regular brunches with my friends. I don't want them to feel like I don't care about them, or that I've cast them aside for you. They'll be impressed that you cooked for them, being that you're a big star and all."

He laughed. "It's the only thing I know how to make, but I wanted to do something to show them, to show you . . ."

"What?" she asked, wrapping her arms around his waist.

"How much you mean to me," he said, kissing her softly. "I know what it's been like lately with all the frantic work on the album, and I don't want you to feel like you have to abandon your life to be with me."

"I don't."

"So, you told me Sara's a film studies professor. What does Troy do?"

"He's a comic book artist, incredibly talented. I think his work is visionary, totally breaks the mold. He works as an illustrator for a publisher to pay the bills, but he also does some of his own stuff. He's had a couple of gallery shows, and he recently released a solo book." She walked over to the coffee table and picked up a large hardcover book with gold trim. Dee brought it to Rye, who was garnishing the plates with cilantro. She said, "This is his work."

He dried his hands on a dish towel and took the tome, flipping slowly through the pages. "Wow, he's really talented. There's so much movement in the images. Bold. Powerful stuff."

"Yeah, and he's a total doll. Just the sweetest guy, wickedly funny in a naughty way I adore."

"You said you met Sara in grad school. How'd you meet Troy?"

"That's a funny story. It was five years ago, just after I bought this place. I went to a gallery opening, some experimental artist. It was wild, basically just stacks of broken glass. I was looking at the largest display when this gorgeous Black man came up beside me. He said, 'What do you think?' Well, you know me, I always try to see the good in all art, so I said, 'It's not necessarily aesthetically pleasing, but I suppose it's interesting. What do you think?' and he said, 'Love, I think it's a heap of shit.' I giggled and he laughed. The next thing I knew, we were having dinner and a pitcher of margaritas at Blue Plate Taco overlooking the Santa Monica Pier. We've been the best of friends ever since."

Rye smiled.

"I've always been kind of a loner because I'm shy and a bit of an introvert. If it weren't for my friends, I'd probably spend all my time alone, doing research, writing, reading. Until you came along, that is."

He ran his finger down the side of her face, and they kissed.

Dee took a breath and continued, "Troy and Sara are like oil and water, but in a playful way. Secretly, they love each other. Sometimes I think they need each other too; they're so different."

"And yet both have devoted themselves to art in their own way," Rye remarked.

"True. Most of my friends are artists or scholars. Creative types. Thinkers. I find being around people like that to be endlessly inspiring."

"Baby, there's no one more inspiring than you."

She blushed. "I'm glad Billy and Susan can join us. I really like them. I'm looking forward to getting to know them better."

He took her hand and said, "They're crazy about you. Billy told me that Susan said she wants you to be her new bestie. Be prepared: she's persistent. She was blown away by how you handled Oliver Spence."

Dee giggled. "That was just luck."

"No, it wasn't," he insisted, kissing her forehead. "Okay, anything left to do before they arrive?"

"Would you help me with the peaches? They need to be peeled, cut in half, and pitted. Then I'll get them blended up so we can make Bellinis, or peach fizzies for those who don't want alcohol."

"You always go the extra mile to make things special and to make sure that everyone is included. It's so sweet. Yet another thing I love about you," he said, staring into her eyes and playing with her hair.

She smiled, picked up a peach, and said, "I'll peel, you cut."

—

"Everyone can go get comfortable outside," Rye said. "I just need to know who wants spicy and who doesn't."

"Mild for me, please," Sara said.

"The spicier, the better," Troy replied. "I like things hot."

Dee giggled. "Of course you do."

"Not spicy for both of us," Billy said.

Dee stayed behind to help Rye assemble and carry the plates. When everyone was served, the hosts took their places at either end of the table. Dee lifted her flute and said, "A toast to friends, and to Rye for making this delicious meal for us."

"Cheers!" everyone said, raising their glasses.

"It was so nice of you to cook for us," Troy said.

"Save your appreciation until you try it," Rye joked.

Dee took a bite. "It's great, honey."

Billy casually glanced at Rye and smiled.

"Sara, Dee tells me you're a film studies professor at UCLA," Rye said. "What kind of films do you focus on in your classes?"

Sara wiped the corners of her mouth and carefully balanced her fork on the edge of her plate. "Mostly contemporary films, both domestic and foreign. My preference tends to be for indie films. I heard that you and William, I mean Billy, are doing a film with Oliver Spence. He's a wonderful director. I teach some of his work in my classes. My students love his modern, fresh take."

"We're excited about it. It's the first time working with him for both of us," Rye said. "Do you study film in your research as well?"

Sara nodded. "I'm working on a series of articles about French cinema over the past forty years. Actually, Dee got me interested in it, making me watch all these crazy French films."

Dee giggled. "Jean Mercier is my favorite filmmaker. Although these days, he does everything in English."

Rye smiled widely. "He's only the most controversial filmmaker of his time."

"Fearless. That's how I see his work," Dee said.

"No one works the way he does," Susan added. "He doesn't allow actors to block or rehearse scenes. In fact, he hates acting altogether!" They all laughed.

"It's true," Susan continued. "Seasoned actors come back from his shoots saying they had no idea what they were doing."

Dee smiled. "It's because he wants them to unlearn. He's trying to make them forget everything they know, because he understands that like muscle memory for a musician or dancer, the tools they need will still be there. He wants them to find the truth in the moment. He wants them to make it real. He doesn't make movies—he makes cinema, art."

Rye gazed lovingly at Dee, unable to take his eyes off her, as usual.

"I agree," Sara replied. "Although to be honest, I find his stuff hard to watch. Some of it is, well, it's aggressive, vulgar."

"I'll drink to that," Troy said, sipping his Bellini.

"He's a real artist, for sure," Billy added. "And a bit of a perv. I get the feeling that he's just trying to see what he can get away with in his sex scenes. I suspect he's having a good laugh at us all."

"He'd probably take that as a compliment," Susan said. "He wants to challenge people."

"That's why he takes on such lofty topics: love, sex, death. Fearless!" Dee said.

"Speaking of fearless," Troy started, "Dee, I just read the manuscript for your forthcoming novella. Brava!"

"You liked it?"

"Loved it, but you know they're going to call you a pornographer."

"It's about time," Dee joked.

Everyone laughed.

"It gave me an idea, actually," Troy said.

"A pornographic idea?" Dee asked.

"No, love, an artistic idea. What would you think about a collaboration? I want to adapt your novella into a graphic novel."

"You want to illustrate *that*? Then they'll call you the pornographer," Dee joked.

Everyone laughed so hard they were nearly falling out of their chairs.

"Pornographer is just a label, like artist or educator," Troy jested, shooting Sara a sarcastic look. Sara rolled her eyes as the others chuckled. When everyone settled down, he continued, "I'm serious. What do you think?"

"It would be a dream," Dee said. "Comics are one of my favorite art forms."

"Why is that?" Rye asked.

"I like art that does something different, that stretches the boundaries or attempts something wholly new. Comics do that by design. By merging words and images, they create a new, distinct language all their own. They even have their own set of conventions, like speech bubbles. But what really fascinates me is how people experience comics differently than any other art form. In a single moment, we experience a comic both as a whole and sequentially. To me, that makes them inherently special, outside the box," Dee replied.

"We must burn the box, love. People need the wood," Troy said.

Dee smiled widely.

"Do you think your publisher will go for it?" Troy asked.

"I'm meeting my editor when Rye and I are in New York. I'll ask her about it. I only want to do it if I can guarantee you'll have total creative freedom." She paused. "Oh, I'm excited just thinking about it. We would have so much fun working together!"

"Oodles," Troy agreed.

Susan playfully said, "So you'll let him adapt one of your books into a graphic novel, but you won't let my production company adapt it into a film. We're going to have to work on that. Let's have lunch when you get back from New York. Don't worry, contrary to what people think, I *can* take no for an answer."

"No, you can't," Billy countered.

Susan teasingly punched his arm and then returned her attention to Dee. "Don't listen to my husband. I think we're going to be fast friends."

Dee glanced at Rye and smiled. He winked in return and said, "There's plenty more of everything in the kitchen. Who wants seconds?"

After everyone left and they finished cleaning up, Dee and Rye went outside to soak up the briny sea air. They lay together on a lounge chair, tangled in an embrace.

"Your friends are great," Rye said.

"They said the same about you on their way out."

"Even Sara?"

"Yeah, and she's a tough critic. She could see how happy I am with you. It was so sweet that you went out of your way to get to know them."

He leaned his head against hers. "Troy's hysterical."

"I know. He keeps me on my toes."

"That's a cool idea he had about collaborating."

"Oh my God, right? I can't believe my good fortune that a talented artist would have an interest in what I do." She paused thoughtfully, and then added, "Rye, when we were chatting with everyone over brunch, I felt so incredibly grateful, so fortunate. I have everything I could ever want. I don't remember ever feeling this way before."

"I was thinking the same thing," he said, pulling her closer.

11

As THE END CREDITS ROLLED, DEE TURNED TO RYE, HER
eyes brimming with tears. She sniffled and said, "I'm so glad Seymour
invited us to watch that. Goodness, it was beautiful. Did you like it?"

He used his thumbs to gently wipe away her tears. "Yes. It was
terrific. Great performances, and the cinematography was breathtaking." He kissed her gently on the forehead, lingering for a moment to
feel close to her. Just then, the lights turned on and Seymour came
barreling in.

"Well, what'd you think?" he asked.

"Delicious popcorn and a sublime film. Bravo!" Dee said, jumping up to hug him. "I was even crying at the end. Such a heartwarm-
ing story. Thank you for letting us watch it."

"You knocked it out of the park, Seymour. It's a winner.
Congratulations," Rye added, reaching out to shake his hand.

"I think so too, but sometimes when you're close to something
and everyone around you is invested in it, you need an honest read.
I can always count on you, Dee," he said, squeezing her shoulders.
"Tell me, do you have notes? Don't be shy."

She shook her head. "Not a single one. It's wonderful."

"Rye, did Dee tell you that she's been giving me advice since she
was a little girl?" Seymour asked. Not waiting for a response, he continued, "It started when she was about six years old. Rose and I were
visiting family in New York, and while we were there, we took Dee

and her folks to a Broadway show, a cheerful musical. Afterward, Dee was crying, absolutely sobbing hysterically. I bent down and asked her, 'Why are you crying?' and I'll never forget, she said, 'Because I loved it so much my heart can't hold all my feelings.'" He stopped to shake his head. "This one loves art with the purest heart of anyone I've ever known."

Rye smiled and traced his finger along Dee's spine, and she looked down, blushing.

"There are no good delis in LA, so after the show, we went to Friedman's. Dee, Rose, and I all ordered matzo ball soup and blintzes," Seymour said.

Dee smiled wistfully. "And my parents shared a pastrami sandwich. My mom always gave my dad the bigger piece."

"That's right," Seymour said. "I asked you about the show and you proceeded to recount every single detail as if you'd memorized it. No one could believe how much you'd absorbed."

"I'd never seen anything like it before."

"Six months later, she and her folks visited us in LA. After seeing how much she had enjoyed the show, I thought it would be fun for her to go to an active movie set. She strolled through the set as if she owned the place, quietly pointing out the pieces of scenery she didn't think looked good. She didn't realize the implications of what she was saying, but she was spot on. This one has always had an eye, a talent, for seeing how the details of a piece of art contribute to the whole. That night, I told her father, 'Lou, your daughter is gifted. Expose her to as much art as you can.' And he agreed." Dee looked down, uncomfortable with too much praise, and bit her lip. "I've been coming to her for advice ever since. When she was twelve, she stayed with us for her spring break. She came to the office with me, and I got called in to see the rough cut of a film we were working on. It was family friendly, and since I didn't want to stick her with my assistant, I brought her along. At the end, I asked her what she thought. She casually said, 'I loved it, but the music didn't go with the story.' I couldn't believe it. She nailed it! The score wasn't right. Only twelve years old," he remarked, shaking his head. "We revamped it, and the film went on to win an Oscar for Best Original Score. She set us on the right path."

"Seymour, you're embarrassing me," Dee said quietly.

"Ha! Well, that's nothing new. Ryder, between us, I get credit for discovering a lot of new talent, but the one I'm proudest of is little Dee. She's always been my Dorothy with a ruby-red heart. I used to worry that our Land of Oz would corrupt her, as it does so many, but the opposite has happened: her pure heart is a mirror to us all. Such a pleasure it's been to see what she's done in her own work." Rye smiled proudly and Seymour continued, "Come on, let's get out of here. Rose gave the cook the night off; she's been in the kitchen all day preparing a feast. Since you drove here, follow me in your car."

"I'll tell you—I've worked with Seymour before, and his reputation is well-earned. He doesn't care much for other people's opinions, but he hangs on your every word," Rye said as they drove through the most elite part of Beverly Hills.

"When I was a kid, he was the only adult who spoke to me like I was an equal. I loved that about him." Dee paused thoughtfully. "It's funny—because of our long history, I think I've seen a side of him that most people in the industry haven't. In some ways, it's like seeing that the great and powerful Wizard of Oz is really just an old man with a smoke machine," she explained.

"How so?"

"Well, when I was sixteen, I spent the summer with them before I left for college. He let me tag along to the studio whenever I wanted. He'd always say, 'We're off to the Emerald City.' One day, I sat in on a meeting he had regarding a film the studio was releasing. The details are a blur after all these years, but it had something to do with appeasing advertisers and making some concessions on the content. After the meeting, he looked me straight in the eyes and said, 'Dee, I'm the luckiest man I know, but there's always a price. Don't ever become like me. Don't ever worry about demographics or corporate interests. There's no place for it in art, only in entertainment. Outside opinion is the death of art. Keep your heart pure and it will never betray you.' Those words are seared into my memory and have guided my practice."

"Wow. I'm floored."

"He's a remarkable man. It was the best advice I've ever received. It's probably why I've never been impressed by the Hollywood thing or by what's popular."

"That's so different from what people in my field see when they look at the great Seymour Peretz," Rye said.

"My dad told me that he fell completely in love with filmmaking when he was a young boy. He saved his pennies and worked odd jobs to pay for movie tickets. He saw cinema as magic and wanted to be its wizard. He came to California to make his dream a reality."

"He sure has done that."

Dee shrugged. "Maybe. There's been a steep price. Filmmaking isn't always romantic. Gold isn't always born from gold dust. To be successful, he's had to make compromises, like a politician; even if they start out with pure intentions, they inevitably get their hands dirty. No one ever imagines that their idealism will fade to black. I think it's why he and I have stayed close. I'm a reminder of home, of his simple dream to make art. He's the Wizard of Oz and he sees me as his Dorothy."

"In all the years I've known Seymour, this is the first time we've hung out socially. Award shows and cast parties aren't the same, and he only ever pops in for a quick appearance," Rye said as he pulled up to the security gate outside the palatial estate.

As the gates opened, Dee remarked, "I remember coming here as a child, how magical it was."

Rye grabbed her hand and said, "I bet," as they drove down the long, winding private drive.

"Just wait until you see their house—it's incredible. When I was little, I thought it was haunted, but not in a bad way, like friendly spirits or something, probably because there's nothing like this in Manhattan, at least nothing I'd ever seen. It was like something out of a book or a movie. I used to roam from room to room, daydreaming. They have the most wonderful art, starting with the fountain and statues outside the front entrance. For a while, I actually believed that they lived in a museum, and thought how lucky that made them."

Rye laughed as he parked the car. He took her hand, lifted it to his lips, and kissed it before they got out. Seymour opened the door before they could knock, revealing the black-and-white marble foyer, high ceilings, an extravagant crystal chandelier, and a grand, golden staircase. "Doesn't it look like something out of *Alice in Wonderland*?" she whispered to Rye. He smiled and squeezed her hand. "Oh my God, it smells like my mother," she said just as Rose came hurrying in.

"Dee! I'm so happy to see you," she said, wrapping her in an enthusiastic hug.

"Oh, I'm so happy to see you too."

"It's been too long. I was overjoyed when Seymour told me you're here full-time now. We can spend lots of time together."

"I'd love that."

When they finally parted, Rose turned to Rye and said, "Ryder, it's nice to see you again. Welcome to our home."

"Thank you for having me," he replied.

"Something smells amazingly familiar," Dee said.

"It's your mother's brisket with all the trimmings."

Dee sniffled and wiped her eyes. "That was so thoughtful of you. Thank you, Rose. I always feel so close to her when I'm here."

"I think of her every day," Rose said. "I'm glad I can give you a little piece of her. Now come on, kids, let's go get settled in the living room." She turned to her husband. "You can get everyone drinks."

Seymour and Rose led the way. Rye put his arm around Dee and whispered, "Are you okay, sweetheart?"

"Yeah. It's just that being here always reminds me of her."

He kissed the side of her head, and they headed to the living room.

"Thank you," Rye said as Seymour handed him a whiskey on the rocks.

"Oh, wow. Rye, come look at these," Dee said, admiring the framed photographs on the mantel. "These pictures are so old."

"Are those your parents with Seymour and Rose?" Rye asked.

"Yup. Lou and Lisette Schwartz at their happiest."

"She was very beautiful," Rye noted. "I've only seen a couple of pictures at your place where she's dressed more casually."

"I think they were going to some black-tie event in that one," Dee said. "Maybe one of Seymour's premieres."

"Is this you with your parents?" Rye asked, picking up a framed photo.

"Uh-huh. I remember it like it was yesterday. Seymour took that when we went to see the Hollywood sign. Here's one just of me," Dee said, taking another photograph down from the mantel. "I was twelve or so. Rose took this when I was sitting out back, reading under this gorgeous lemon tree they have. I didn't even know she took it at the time." She became misty.

"What is it, sweetheart?" he asked softly.

"I was still so sad back then. That's why my nose was constantly in a book. For a long time, art was the only way to escape the loneliness."

He kissed her forehead.

"Well, enough of that," she said, wiping her eyes and putting the photograph back. "Now I have you."

He smiled and kissed her again, on the lips this time.

"So Dee, what have you been up to since you moved to the Golden State?" Seymour asked.

She and Rye sat on a couch opposite their hosts. "Well, Rye's been working on recording some original songs, and I've been hanging out in the studio with him. I'm also working on a new poetry collection. I have some lectures back East coming up. We're actually flying to Florida tomorrow to see my dad, and then we'll continue on to New York."

"I'm sure Lou's looking forward to the visit."

Before long, they sat down to eat a nostalgic, home-cooked meal. As they finished dinner, Dee remarked, "Rose, that was simply wonderful. It was just like my mother used to make. It means so much to me."

"It was my pleasure," she replied, smiling warmly. "Now, I know you actors never eat sweets, but Ryder, I've made Lisette's apple cake and you have to try it."

"I wouldn't pass that up," Rye said.

"You really didn't have to go to all this trouble," Dee said.

Rose smiled and said, "No trouble at all. Besides, it makes me feel close to her too. I just love having you here." The staff came in and began clearing the dishes. Rose stood up. "I'm going to check on dessert. We can eat it in the living room."

"Please, let me help you," Dee said, rising. "I insist."

Rose smiled. "It will be good to have some time alone together."

When they left the room, Seymour suggested, "Let's head to the other room. Bring your glass and I'll top you off." As he refilled Rye's glass with amber-colored liquid, he said, "So, you're going to meet her father?"

"Yes. Dee said you two grew up together."

"That's right," Seymour replied, handing him his glass and taking the seat opposite him. "We're just a couple of Brooklyn boys who made it big. We weren't even in elementary school yet when we first met, just neighborhood kids. We'd play stoop ball, go to the park, and save our pennies for the ice cream truck. We became best friends." He stopped to laugh. "A lot of the kids in our neighborhood didn't imagine much for their lives beyond what their folks had. Lou was different. I was too. He was fiercely practical and I was a bit of a dreamer, but we both made big plans for our lives, worked our asses off, and saw them through. Eventually I moved out here, but we'd visit one another often. Rose and Lisette hit it off like two peas in a pod, and so we always stayed in each other's lives. Not a lot of people can say that about a childhood friend, especially around here."

"No, I imagine not."

"Ryder, Lou is an old-fashioned guy. Dee is his only child and he's understandably protective of her. Nothing means more to him than she does. Family is everything to him, and she's all he's got left. He's a real salt-of-the-earth kind of man. And Dee loves him to the moon and back."

Rye looked at him intently.

"He called me after those paparazzi caught you two kissing outside that restaurant. He asked if I knew you and what I thought." He paused before adding, "I vouched for you. I told him you're a good man and that he shouldn't believe the press."

"Thank you. I appreciate that."

"I wouldn't have said it if I didn't believe it. I know you've had your, well, whatever you want to call them when you were younger. But I trust that it's all in the past. Dee deserves the best."

Rye took a breath and said, "Seymour, I love Dee. I love her with all my heart."

Seymour smiled. "I can see that. The way you two look at each other is great to witness. Rose and I are thrilled. She was so consumed by sadness after her mother passed. It's only now I see it lifting, obviously in no small part thanks to you. But Lou may need a little more convincing than that."

"What are you saying?" Rye asked.

"You need to do this right. Show your respect for him, for his daughter, and for their relationship. Fame won't impress him, and neither will money. He wants to make sure that his daughter ends up with a quality young man." He stopped to smile and said, "You'll be okay. But Ryder, do this thing the right way, the respectful way."

Rye nodded. "I will. You have my word. I love her, Seymour; if he's important to her, he's important to me. Thank you."

Just then, Rose and Dee returned and passed out plates with slices of apple cake and a dollop of fresh whipped cream. The smell of cinnamon swirled in the room. Dee sat down and Rye draped his arm around her. She took a bite of the cake and mumbled, "Oh my God."

"I hope I did your mother's recipe justice. How does it taste?" Rose asked.

"It tastes like love," Dee replied.

12

"WE'VE REACHED OUR CRUISING ALTITUDE," THE PILOT announced.

Rye unclipped his seat belt, took Dee's hand, and said, "Come here," leading her to a leather couch. They lay down side by side, and he wrapped his arms around her.

"This feels so good," he said.

"I still can't believe you chartered a jet. You didn't need to do something so extravagant," she insisted.

"It's our first trip together, and I wanted it to be special."

"Honey, it's special because we're together."

He smiled and kissed her softly. "You're the sweetest person I've ever known." She blushed and he ran his fingers along her cheek. "I mean it. I love you and I don't ever want to let you go."

"Good. I love you too, more than I thought was possible."

He kissed her again and said, "Tell me more about your father. I'm actually pretty nervous about meeting him. It's like an audition I can't prepare for."

"There's no reason to be nervous. He can't wait to meet you."

"I know how important he is to you, and I want him to like me."

"He will like you. He'll see how we feel about each other, and that's all that matters to him. Besides, you don't have a lot of competition. He never cared for anyone else I dated."

Rye laughed and said, "Somehow that doesn't make me feel better."

"With Jett, he thought he'd drag me down, that I'd never live up to my potential if we stayed together. He saw him as deadweight, unreliable, unmotivated. Begged me to break it off. In the end, he wasn't wrong."

"What about Russell? I'd think an investment banker would be impressive to most fathers."

"Not mine. He's never been impressed by success in the abstract. He respects hard work, integrity, passion, and loyalty. It's not about money or job titles. He would have been fine with Russell if he thought I loved him, but he knew I didn't. He always told me, 'Aspire to greatness in life and love, and never forget who you are.' My parents were crazy about each other and he wanted me to have the same thing, or at least not close off the possibility. That's precisely why he'll adore you," she said, brushing her fingers across his temple.

"Dee, it's just . . ."

"What?"

"You told me how much your father values education. I dropped out of school when I was fourteen years old to pursue acting. How's he going to feel about his only daughter being with someone who didn't even graduate high school?"

"Honey, he's not like that. He's the least snooty person you'll ever meet. While he fancies himself an intellectual, he's nothing like the stereotype you might have in mind. He respects all learning, not just formal education. You are smart, well-read, talented, and incredibly accomplished. You spend your life doing what you love—that's admirable. There's nothing to be nervous about. Besides, he'll see what a good man you are, how much you love me."

He pressed his forehead to hers and whispered, "I just want to do everything right with you, with us. It's important to me."

"Just when I think I can't love you more," she whispered.

He pulled back, took her face in his hands, and kissed her.

"Sundays were really special when I was growing up. Maybe it's the best way for you to understand the kind of man my dad is."

"Tell me."

"Well, he worked a lot, but he always made time for family. Every Sunday, he took me out for breakfast, just the two of us. My mother liked to sleep in, so we'd go out alone, and then pick up my mother afterward and all spend the day together. Those breakfasts were the highlight of my week. We went to delis and diners where every host, waitress, and regular knew his name. From the moment we walked through the front door, he'd be greeting everyone and catching up like they were all old pals. He's friendly with everyone, a real people person. Funny too. Classic jokester. Anyway, I'd usually order blintzes or potato pancakes. At my favorite place, I always ordered blueberry pancakes. They came with this amazing blueberry sauce, sticky and sweet. My dad always asked them to bring me extra on the side because I liked it so much."

Rye smiled. "That's sweet."

"Yeah. My mother died on a Tuesday. The following Sunday, I was in my room, lying in bed with one of my dolls, unspeakably sad." Rye rubbed her arm and she continued, "My dad knocked on my bedroom door. When he opened it, I saw he was dressed from head to toe, with his coat and hat on. He said, 'You're not ready yet?' I just looked at him and muttered, 'I didn't know we were still going.' He smiled and said, 'Get dressed and brush your teeth. I'll be waiting in the living room.' After we ordered breakfast, he tried talking to me about school or something banal. I remember saying, 'I'm too sad to talk,' and he said, 'That's okay.

We can just sit together and eat.' So we did. After breakfast, he took me to Central Park and then to a bookstore. From that Sunday on, we'd go to breakfast and then he'd take me somewhere for the day, usually a museum or the public library, which was my favorite."

"Why was that your favorite?"

"Because it was quiet. We could be together, reading, without uttering a single word."

He leaned his forehead against hers and then kissed her gently. "He sounds like a great father."

"He is. He was devastated when my mother died, which is why he never remarried, I suppose. He does have a girlfriend now, Dolly, who you'll meet. He calls her his 'lady friend,' which is kind of funny. She has big, platinum hair and smells like she took a bath in drugstore perfume, but she's very sweet and they're adorable together."

Rye smiled.

"See the thing is, no matter how heartbroken he was, he kept living and made sure I kept living too. That's the core of who he is: an optimist who always shows up for the people he loves. You have nothing to be nervous about. You're an extraordinary man, and I've never been happier. My dad has a way of focusing on what really matters."

He kissed her forehead and said, "I've never been happier either."

When they walked through the arrival door at the airport, Dee spotted her father immediately. He was wearing white shorts and a blue-and-white-striped polo shirt that showed off his tanned skin. He grinned from ear to ear, opened his arms, and jubilantly called, "Deanna Banana!" She ran to hug him.

"Hi, Daddy," she whispered. "I missed you so much." When they eventually parted, Dee said, "Daddy, this is Rye."

"It's a pleasure to meet you, sir," Rye said, extending his hand.

"Please call me Lou. Very nice to meet you. Welcome to Delray Beach," he said, giving him a hearty handshake. "Let me help with your luggage," he added, grabbing the handle of one of the suitcases.

Rye turned to the porter, slipped him a twenty-dollar bill, and said, "We're all set, thank you." He lifted his guitar case by the handle and wheeled the other suitcase, following Lou outside.

"This place is only for private planes. I've never been here before," Lou said as they loaded up the trunk of his white Mercedes. "How was the flight?"

"Terrific. Fast and easy," Dee replied.

"I figured you two might be hungry. How about we stop at the Club House for a late lunch?"

"That sounds great," Rye said, slipping into the back seat. He leaned forward and squeezed Dee's shoulder. She put her hand on his, serenity on her face.

Lou noticed the subtle show of affection, smiled to himself, and drove off.

When they arrived at the Club House inside Lou's gated community, the hostess said, "Mr. Schwartz. You missed lunch with your crew. They're just finishing up."

"Evelyn, this is my daughter, Dee. She's visiting with her friend," Lou replied.

"How wonderful. It's lovely to meet you both." She then looked more carefully at Rye, did a double take, and said, "Uh, where would you like to sit today, Mr. Schwartz?"

"Outside in the shade, please."

Dee and Rye held hands as Evelyn led them to their table. They passed a large group of men whose dishes were being cleared. Lou stopped and said, "Fellas, you all remember my daughter, Dee."

"Hello," she said.

They all offered friendly greetings.

"Your dad hasn't stopped talking about your visit," one of them said. "It's a good thing you're here; otherwise, he'd be swindling us in a card game tonight."

"He is a trickster," Dee replied. "You guys are on your own with him."

Lou laughed and said, "Donald, you just need to learn to read the room."

"Speaking of reading, Dee, your last book was a page-turner. Very funny, and some pretty raunchy stuff," Donald added.

"It was sweet of you to read it. Thank you," she replied.

"Hey, what's this book you're talking about? I'd like to read it," another elderly man said.

"You're not old enough," Lou joked. "There are adult themes. Get back to me next month when you turn eighty."

Rye laughed and Lou said, "Everyone, this is Dee's friend, Rye Field. Rye, this group of troublemakers is the Brooklyn Eight." He pointed to a short man at the end of the table and said, "Morty over there is from Queens, but we don't hold it against him."

"Yes, you do," Morty replied.

They all laughed.

"Nice to meet you all," Rye said.

"Hey, you look familiar. You're that actor, Ryder Field," one of the men said. "Lou, you didn't tell us Dee was dating a big star."

"That's right. I used to watch *The Mission* every week," another chimed in.

Rye looked down, blushing.

"I watched it too. Great show. Of course, anyone would be lucky to be with my Deanna Banana," Lou said. "See you guys later."

When they sat down, the hostess took their drink order—iced teas all around—and handed them each a menu. "They'll make you anything you want. They're very accommodating. The tuna salad is great; so is the Cobb salad," Lou said. "If you feel like something unhealthy, they have grilled Hebrew National hot dogs. I indulge a couple of times a year."

"God, I haven't eaten one of those since I was a kid," Dee said. "Is Dolly joining us?"

"She didn't want to interfere with our catching up, so she's getting her hair done. She'll join us for dinner tonight. I figured you kids might be tired after your trip, so I planned to barbecue at the house, if that's okay. I made us reservations for tomorrow night. Does Italian work?"

"Sounds great," Dee said.

"Yes, that sounds perfect. Thank you," Rye said. As they perused the menu, Rye touched Dee's hand. "Sweetheart, what are you having?"

Lou kept his eyes down but smiled to himself at the tenderness between his daughter and her new beau.

After the waitress took their order, Dee asked, "So, Daddy, what are you reading these days?" She turned to Rye and explained, "He's an avid reader."

"I just finished a series of crime novels I really enjoyed. A little formulaic but light, easy reading. Next, I think I'll switch back to nonfiction. I'm planning to dive into that recent book about how Abraham Lincoln got into politics."

"I read that one," Rye said. "Learned a lot. It's fascinating, especially if you're an American history buff. It pairs well with the Brown series on the Civil War for a broader perspective. If you haven't read them, I'm sure you'd love them. I did."

"If I could go back, I probably would have studied history in college. What did you study in school?" Lou asked.

Rye glanced at Dee nervously. She gently took his hand under the table and gave it a supportive squeeze. "Regretfully, I didn't finish high school. I dropped out to pursue acting. But I'm fascinated with history and world affairs, so I read as much as I can."

Lou smiled. "I've always thought that a motivated person could get a graduate-level education with just a library card."

Rye's face relaxed and he took a calming breath.

"*The Mission* was one of my favorite shows. I have so many questions," Lou said.

"Ask away," Rye replied, smiling brightly. The conversation continued effortlessly throughout lunch and the short ride to Lou's home.

After unpacking, they spent the day unwinding on Lou's lanai. Late that afternoon, Dee and Rye slipped into the hot tub. Lou glanced up from his book occasionally and noticed Rye's arm slung around Dee, joy on his daughter's face as they whispered to each other. That night, Dolly came over with a big salad and even bigger hair. Lou grilled chicken and steak, and they all ate outside under a canopy of white paper lanterns. At Dee's urging, Rye treated them to some music on his acoustic guitar, which they all enjoyed.

The next day, all four went out to breakfast, followed by a stroll around the Morikami Museum and Japanese Gardens. Dee and Rye walked hand in hand. They stopped in front of an exhibit of small figurines, examining the exquisite collection. Rye stood behind Dee, his hands wrapped lovingly around her waist as she leaned onto him. Lou watched from a distance.

Later that evening, they went to Lou's favorite Italian restaurant for dinner, where he was greeted by the maître d' like an old friend. Over dinner, Rye riveted the group with stories about movies he'd worked on, and Dee caught them up on her latest research. At the end of the meal, Dolly ordered tiramisu. Just as it was served, a trio of musicians began playing Sinatra, and they opened up a small dance floor.

"Mmm, this is delicious," Dolly said, taking a bite of her dessert. She pushed the plate forward. "Please, have some."

"No, thank you," Dee replied.

"None for me either, thank you," Rye said. "I try to avoid sugar."

"I'm sure you actors have to watch everything you eat," Dolly said, pulling the plate back. "I know I'm not exactly a young woman, and I wouldn't want to trouble you, but I've never danced with a movie star before," she added coyly.

Rye smiled, rose, and said, "It would be my pleasure; I'd love to dance with you," as he reached for her hand.

Once they were on the dance floor and out of earshot, Dee turned to her father. "Well? What do you think?"

"He's terrific. He brings you out of your shell too. You seem so comfortable with him, like you've known him all your life. You both seem completely at ease with one another."

"I'm in love with him."

Lou smiled. "I can see that. It's obviously mutual. It's what I've always wanted for you, a great love. I'm extremely happy for you. Your mother would have been too."

Dee's eyes became teary. She sniffled and said, "Thank you. He was nervous about meeting you. Your opinion means the world to me."

"I've only ever wanted your happiness. Never settle, Dee. Aspire to greatness in life and love."

She smiled. "I am."

"And never forget who you are."

"I won't."

"Now, how about we get up and join them? Let your old dad take his little girl for a spin around the dance floor," he said, rising.

Dolly was saying something to Rye, and he laughed as he whirled her around. He caught Dee's eye as she danced with her father and winked.

As Dee was packing the next morning, Rye walked over and said, "Hey, come here." He put his arms around her, holding her in his strong embrace.

"Being in your arms feels so good," she whispered.

He pulled back and kissed her softly. "I love you with all my heart."

She rested her head against his chest, feeling enveloped in both his arms and his love. "Thank you for coming here with me. It means more to me than I can express."

He kissed the top of her head. "Next time we'll stay longer. I know it wasn't nearly enough. I'm gonna go get some coffee while you finish up."

"Okay," she said. "But kiss me again first."

He smiled and kissed her passionately.

"Rye?" she whispered.

"Yeah, sweetheart?"

"I love you too, with all my heart."

He kissed her once more and then meandered toward the kitchen.

"Good morning. I'm just putting the coffee on," Lou said. "Can I get you something for breakfast?"

"Good morning. No, thank you. Just coffee will be fine. I was actually hoping to speak with you privately for a moment."

"Sure," Lou replied, walking toward the living room. "Let's have a seat."

Lou plopped down in his recliner, and Rye sat facing him on the couch. Rye sat with perfectly upright posture, looked him straight in the eyes, and said, "Lou, I want you to know how much I love your daughter."

Lou smiled. "I'm glad to hear that."

"And I want to tell you my intentions."

As they stood in the airport lobby, Rye instructed the porter to go ahead with their luggage while they said their goodbyes.

"Rye, it was great meeting you. I look forward to seeing you again," Lou said as he extended his hand.

"Likewise," Rye said, shaking his hand. "Thank you for everything."

"You two have a great time in New York. Dee, knock 'em dead at your talks."

She smiled sorrowfully. "I'm so sad to leave you. This was far too short."

"Next time we'll make it longer. Dolly and I have been talking about taking a vacation— what if we visited you guys in LA? It would be a chance to see Seymour and Rose too."

Dee's face lit up. "I would love that."

"We both would," Rye added.

"Well, give me a hug for the road, my little Deanna Banana."

Dee giggled and hugged her father tightly. "Thank you for everything," she whispered.

"Be happy," he whispered back.

When they finally parted, she said, "Bye, Daddy. I love you."

"Love you too," he replied.

Lou watched as Rye put his arm around Dee. She nuzzled against him, and they headed toward the jet.

13

"WE'RE RIGHT BY CENTRAL PARK," DEE SAID EXCITEDLY as Rye checked them into the Four Seasons.

"Mr. Field, please allow me to personally escort you to your suite," the manager said. "The bellmen will follow with your luggage."

Rye took Dee's hand, and they all walked to a private elevator. The manager hit the button for the fifty-second-floor penthouse. "This is your elevator," he said. "I'll be available to you twenty-four hours a day for anything you may need."

Dee looked at Rye and furrowed her brow.

"The penthouse is 4,300 square feet, and as you'll see, it has a 360-degree view of the city," the manager explained. "There are four glass balconies where you can sit and enjoy meals, each offering a view of a different part of the city." He turned to Rye. "Sir, the chauffeured Rolls-Royce that picked you up at the airport is at your disposal for the duration of your stay."

Dee looked at Rye, her eyes wide. The elevator slowed as it reached the top, and the doors opened directly into a palatial luxury suite. The manager said, "Please, after you."

Dee gasped at the extravagance that unfolded all around her. She slowly turned in a circle, taking in the opulent surroundings, trying to catch her breath. Rye smiled and squeezed her wrist. "I can't believe you did this," she muttered. The manager showed them around the spectacular penthouse, pointing out the exquisite sculptures and paintings, the hand-lacquered walls with mother-of-pearl inlay, the special collection of books about art and culture, the Zen room, the private spa, and the infinity bathtub with fiber-optic lighting and massage jets that over-looked Central Park. When he left, Dee strolled into the library. She craned her neck to look at all the books, shelved high to the ceiling. She ran her hand along the baby grand piano. Rye came up behind her and slipped his hands around her waist, planting kisses all along her neck. She leaned back into him and whispered, "I can't believe you did this."

"I wanted to do something special for you, something romantic."

"All I want is to be with you. Really, I don't need anything else."

"Sweetheart, that just makes me want to do special things for you even more. I know you don't care about material things, but I picked this penthouse because it's famous for the library and all the art. You told me that you loved going to the public library and art museums when you were little; this was the closest I could get."

She spun to face him, tears in her eyes. "It's the sweetest, most magical thing anyone's ever done for me."

He gently wiped her tears and kissed her softly. "I know you, and I love you with all my heart."

She rested her head on his chest. "I love you too. I always will."

"Last night was sublime," Dee said, leaning her head on Rye's shoulder as the car whizzed through the city. "Theater and sushi in my favorite city with the man of my dreams. Doesn't get better."

He kissed the top of her head. "Not to mention the good use we made of the hotel suite."

She giggled.

"It was a terrific show. Incredible performances," he said. "It was so cute the way you cried at the end, even though it was happy."

"I can't help it. I've always been that way, crying at the beginning, the end, or anytime the art moves me. I'm so glad we were able to see that last night. Experiencing art always motivates me before I give a lecture." She looked up at him and said, "You're so sweet to come with me today," as the car approached Columbia University, their final stop of the day.

"I wouldn't miss it for the world," Rye replied, holding her hand. "I couldn't be more blown away. Your lectures have been brilliant. Everyone has been so inspired, me included."

She blushed.

"You make people believe in the power of art." He squeezed her hand. "I've spent my entire life working as an actor, but it's only in listening to you that I'm able to see it anew. You've changed the way I think about my own work and the projects I want to tackle."

"Rye, if you follow your heart and your gut, you'll always make the right choices."

"You must be exhausted, three schools in one day."

"It's a lot, but each talk fuels me—the exchange of energy between me and the audience. Sometimes it's easier to power through and do them back-to-back. Plus, it gives us a free day tomorrow. I'm so looking forward to spending the day with you. What do you want to do?"

"Anything, sweetheart. I've been here a thousand times, but I've never really explored the city. I want to see New York through your eyes."

"How about a morning stroll through Central Park?" Dee asked. "I love all the street performers. Have you ever been to the Neue Galerie?"

He shook his head.

"We could go there and see Klimt's *Woman in Gold*. They have a terrific café where we can grab a bite. Then maybe the Guggenheim or a walk around Madison Avenue. We could go back to the hotel before the show, then dash down to Times Square. After the show, I'm taking you to a late-night dinner at Friedman's, my favorite deli."

"That sounds perfect."

"But you can't go all LA actor on me and nibble on a kale salad. I'm going to order us the works: matzo ball soup, blintzes, potato pancakes, smoked salmon. Don't worry, you can just try a little of everything."

"Baby, I'm not worried about a thing. I can't wait. Tonight, I'm having room service prepare a special candlelit meal for us. We can eat outside on the balcony and enjoy that jaw-dropping view. Then maybe we can take a steam in the sauna or a swim in that soaker tub. I'll massage your feet and you can just relax."

"That sounds blissful," she said.

"On our last day, I made a dinner reservation at the Metropolitan Museum of Art restaurant."

"Ooh, that's so romantic. Thank you. I'm sorry I'll have to work that afternoon. There was no way I could diplomatically get out of seeing my publisher and agent."

"That's okay, sweetheart. Do what you need to do. I'll be glad to have some quiet time in the hotel room to read through some of those scripts my agent sent over. You'll get back in plenty of time to freshen up and change, and we can head to dinner."

"Rye, I know we just got here last night, but I already know this is going to be the best three days of my life."

He smiled and ran his fingers down the side of her face.

"We're here," the driver announced.

Rye took Dee's hand as they scurried up the stairs outside the Metropolitan Museum of Art and then through the museum, to the elevator, and up to The Dining Room.

"Good evening, Mr. Field," the host said as he promptly escorted them to the best seat in the house: a corner table by the window, overlooking Central Park. He moved to pull out Dee's chair, but Rye said, "I've got it."

"Very good, sir," the host replied, leaving menus on the table.

Rye pulled out Dee's chair and she sat down. He kissed the top of her head before taking his own seat.

"Coming here was a great idea. It's the perfect end to our trip. Such an incredible view," she said, gazing dreamily out the window. "Too bad we couldn't get here earlier so we could see the art."

"After dinner," he replied.

"Honey, the museum's closed."

"I made arrangements. We can see whatever you want."

"Really? That's amazing!" she said, smiling brightly.

"You're amazing," he replied, reaching across the table and taking her hand.

She glanced down, blushing.

He massaged her fingers. "I love you so much."

"I love you too," she said, staring into his eyes.

The waiter approached. "May I start you out with a cocktail or bottle of wine?"

"Sure," Dee said. "Maybe I'll have a glass of wine," she mused, scouring the menu.

"Sweetheart, how about a bottle of champagne instead?" Rye asked.

She smiled. "Okay."

"A bottle of your best champagne," Rye said, handing the waiter the wine list.

"Right away," he replied, darting off.

"This has been such a special trip. I've loved seeing New York through your eyes," Rye said.

"Moving to LA was the right decision for me, but as happy as I've been, especially since meeting you, I do miss New York sometimes. Being here with you has been so romantic. Thank you for coming with me. I'm sorry I had to spend part of the trip working."

"Don't be. I always knew you were brilliant, but hearing you give those lectures, I was completely blown away. Your work is extraordinary. You're really doing something important. And oh my God, when you were firing off answers to the audience's questions, I just couldn't believe how much knowledge you have at your fingertips." She shook her head as if to dismiss his praise, but he pressed on. "I mean it. You're an inspiring speaker. Knowing how quiet you tend to be in crowds, I was taken aback by how plugged in you become."

"You're very sweet. Work has always been different for me, louder I guess, whether it's writing or giving talks. Maybe because when there's something you want to do in the world, it isn't really about you anymore. Something bigger takes center stage and you're just the messenger, so you surrender to that and become a vessel."

The waiter returned, popped open a bottle of champagne, and filled their flutes. "I'll be back momentarily to answer any questions you may have about the menu," he said, walking off.

Rye raised his glass. "To being together and to magic. Cheers."

"Cheers," she said as they clinked glasses.

"Shall we?" he asked, picking up his menu.

"Hmm, everything sounds good. I can't decide between the scallops and the crab cakes."

"Let's get both and share," Rye suggested.

"Great. Do you want to start with a salad to balance out that orgy of unhealthy food we had last night?"

Rye laughed. "Perfect. Let's preorder the chocolate soufflé for dessert. I've heard it's a must."

"You never eat dessert," she replied.

"It's our last night in New York. Let's splurge."

"I won't argue."

Rye signaled the waiter and ordered their meal.

"You're really spoiling me. I could get used to this," Dee said.

"Good. You should."

She blushed. They gazed into each other's eyes, and eventually she said, "My publisher loved Troy's idea about adapting my book into a graphic novel. It's a go. I FaceTimed him on the way back to the hotel. He's so excited. He'll have total creative freedom, which really is the only way a project like this will work."

"Oh, sweetheart, that's wonderful. I have no doubt he'll do something amazing and completely unexpected."

She smiled. "So, what did you think of the scripts you read today?"

For the next hour and a half, they talked nonstop as they enjoyed a decadent meal.

"This is delicious," Dee said, taking a final bite of the soufflé. "I hope the chocolate doesn't keep me up all night."

"I won't complain if it does. I know how we can spend the time," he said with a wink.

She smiled and rolled her eyes playfully. "Are we really allowed to walk around the museum?"

"Anywhere we want. Do you have a favorite piece of art here?"

"Many. There's one I'd love to show you by Georges Seurat. You'll like it. I know where it is."

"Let's save it for last." Rye signed the credit card receipt, rose to his feet, and took Dee's hand. "Shall we see some art?"

They meandered around the museum, hand in hand. At the doorway to each exhibit hall, a guard smiled at them and waved them through. "This is so amazing, having all of this to ourselves," Dee whispered. Rye pecked her cheek. "Have you ever done anything like this before?" she asked.

"Never." He stopped to kiss her before they continued walking. When they arrived in a room featuring a photographic exhibit depicting refugees, they stood solemnly, Rye with his arm around Dee. When they got to the contemporary art wing, Rye whirled her around, and they danced their way through several rooms. She couldn't stop giggling. After visiting a few more exhibits, Rye said, "How about you show me that Seurat?"

"Sure, it's in the Post-Impressionist room. Over there," she said, leading the way.

They arrived at the room and wandered past several works by van Gogh and Gauguin, before reaching *Circus Sideshow* by Seurat. They stopped in front of it, Rye standing behind Dee with his hands around her waist.

"This is the first painting he did portraying popular entertainment. It's the sideshow outside of the circus. Performers would entertain people for free. See," she said, pointing, "those are the people watching. I think it's kind of interesting to think about art and entertainment, to question what they mean and what we value. Like the difference between the street performers we saw the other day, or the graffiti, and the works hanging on these walls. Anyway, I thought you might like it."

"I do. It's terrific," he said, squeezing her.

She turned to face him. He cupped her face in his hands, and they kissed.

"The night we had dinner with Oliver Spence and he was hounding you with adoration, he asked what you were looking for. You said you wanted someone to stroll around a museum with you and just ask you if you enjoyed it. So, did you?"

"Yes," she said.

He kissed her again.

"I'm sorry, but I have to ask one more thing."

She looked down and asked, "What's that?"

He got down on bended knee and held out a ten-carat, emerald-cut diamond ring with a simple platinum band. He grinned and said, "Deanna Schwartz, you make me want to be extraordinary. I love you with all my heart, and I can't imagine spending my life without you. Will you marry me?"

Her eyes flooded. Through her tears, she whispered, "Yes, I'll marry you."

He slipped the ring on her finger, rose, and picked her up off the ground, twirling her around. They were both smiling and giggling when he finally put her down. He cradled her cheek in his hand and kissed her passionately, running his hands through her hair.

"I love you so much," she whispered.

"I love you too, sweetheart."

14

WHEN THEY GOT INTO THEIR PRIVATE ELEVATOR, RYE picked Dee up and said, "I'm carrying you over the threshold."

She giggled. "We just got engaged! We're not married yet," she protested.

"I'm practicing." The elevator door opened, and he carried her to the bedroom and gently laid her down. He crawled into bed next to her, pulled her body close to his, and stared into her eyes with total adoration. He slowly undressed her from head to toe, kissing every inch of her body before pulling off his own clothes. They made love passionately, screaming in ecstasy, and then lay side by side, playing with each other's hair.

"I must be the luckiest man in the world," he said softly.

"I thought I was the lucky one," she replied. She looked at the rock on her finger, sparkling like her eyes, and said, "I thought you never wanted to get married again."

"I didn't. That all changed when I met you."

She smiled and pressed her mouth to his.

"When we were in Florida, I asked your father for his blessing."

"You did?" she asked, tearing up.

He caressed her cheek. "He gave it without reservation. I meant it when I said I want to do everything right with you."

She kissed him again and said, "I love you."

"I love you too, sweetheart. Move in with me when we get back to LA. I know you love being on the beach, but I was hoping . . ."

"Of course I'll move in with you. Your house is magnificent. All I really want is to wake up with you each morning and fall asleep in your arms each night."

"If you're not happy there, we'll sell it and buy something else."

"I'll be happy there. But let's keep my house for weekends or whenever we want a beach escape."

"I had the same thought. When we get back, we'll only have a few days before we have to head to the film location in Montana. I'll hire a crew to move everything for you. Don't worry about anything."

She smiled brightly. "I'm not."

"The shoot will be two and a half months. I was thinking—we could get married as soon as it wraps."

"Really?"

"I don't want to wait a minute longer than we have to. Then we'll have a few weeks to go on a honeymoon, or stay at home, or do whatever you want before the tour. I'll be working long hours between now and then, but we can hire a wedding planner to take care of everything. What kind of wedding do you want?"

"Something intimate. Nothing too big or flashy, okay?"

He kissed her forehead. "Of course. We could have it at our house if you want. We could set up a tent outside, although it might attract the paparazzi."

"How would you feel about asking Seymour and Rose if we could have it at their house? I think they'd be happy to host our celebration, and that way, it would be someplace where . . ."

"Where your mother has been."

She smiled. "No one has ever known me the way you do."

He kissed her gently and said, "That sounds perfect. Go ahead and ask them. Sweetheart, I wanted to talk to you about what my work life is like. I made a lot of mistakes in my first marriage because we never talked about any of it. I foolishly thought that just being married was enough. I don't want to make the same mistakes with you. This has to be a partnership."

"What are you saying?"

"I've been between projects since we met, but I've told you what my life is normally like. When I start the new TV show, things will be pretty stable since we're filming in LA, but even then, if I get a good film script or go on the road again with the band on my hiatuses, I'm worried about our relationship. I'd love for you to come with me, but I respect that you have a life of your own. Your work is so important. I'm in awe of it. Please know I would never let it take a back seat."

"Rye, can I tell you something?"

"Anything, my love."

"I've always had this fantasy of what love would be like, what life could be like. It's simple, really: two people waking up together each day, loving each other, going out into the world and doing their own amazing things, then crawling into bed together at night and falling asleep in each other's arms. That's what I want for us. I want us to always be this close and for each of us to be more of who we are, not less."

"I want that too," he said, stroking her hair. "There's a reason that very little lasts in Hollywood. How do we do this?"

"Smart, caring people can figure almost anything out. With a little planning, we won't have to give up anything. The truth is, most of the time, I can work from anywhere. I'm happy to go on the road with you. New places always inspire me."

"Dee, I need you to know I'm not going to fuck this up. I'm done thinking only of myself. You will come first."

"Honey, I know how ambitious you are and what you hope to accomplish. Acting and music are your calling, your passion. They're a big part of what makes you who you are, and I love who you are. Please don't think you have to choose or construct a hierarchy. There are no limits for your work or mine. We'll do it all together."

He kissed her and said, "I can't wait to marry you."

"Me too."

"We never talked about children. Is that something you want?" he asked.

"Yes, but I've always been scared. Losing my mother so young . . ."

"I know," he said, tucking her hair behind her ear.

"Being an only child was hard too. But I always dreamed of being pregnant, being a mother. What about you?"

"I obviously prioritized my career. If I have my work and I have you, I will be happy, but . . ."

"Yeah?"

"Sweetheart, I would love to have a family with you."

"Really?"

"Yes," he said softly. "I promise I would give it everything. We have the means to figure out how to focus on our children while still pursuing our careers to the extent we want to. We're older than most first-time parents, so there may not be a lot of time. After we get married, maybe we could start trying and just see what happens. What do you think?"

"I think I'm completely in love with you. And even though we're not trying to make a baby quite yet, I think that I absolutely have to have you again. Make love with me."

He smiled, grabbed her, and pulled her on top of him.

15

THE DAY OF THE WEDDING, GUESTS ARRIVED AT SEYMOUR and Rose's estate and were escorted outside to their seats for the ceremony. Seymour had thousands of red poppies flown in from Europe; the wedding canopy was completely covered in the red bursts. The night before the ceremony, Dee slept over and Seymour confessed, "I couldn't let my little Dorothy get married without poppies," to which she replied, "It's absolutely magical."

At Dee's request, they kept the guest list to one hundred people, but nevertheless it was a star-studded affair. Grey and Sloane Hewson arrived looking like Hollywood royalty—Grey, dashing in a black Christian Dior suit, and Sloane, impossible to miss in a red knee-length Valentino dress that matched her pouty lips. Billy and Susan Sumner sat beside them, sporting matching dark sunglasses, the accessory of the day. Troy and Sara came together. Sara marveled at the beautiful surroundings, wondering about the films Seymour had hatched up on those very premises, while Troy ogled the many celebrities in attendance, wondering who might be unattached. Music producer Porter Lewis came with the musicians in Rye's band. He did a double take when he noticed Sara. They made eye contact and she looked down, blushing.

Frederick Field, Rye's father, arrived with French actress Claudette Dubois, thirty years his junior. Wearing a short dress that looked like liquid gold, Claudette caught everyone's eye. They headed straight for Rye, who was chatting with Seymour, Lou, and Dolly.

"Dad, I'm so glad you're here," Rye said, hugging him. "This is Dee's father, Lou Schwartz, and his friend Dolly."

"Pleased to meet you," Lou said, extending his hand.

"Likewise," Frederick replied, shaking his hand.

"I'm a big fan of yours," Dolly said, giggling like a schoolgirl.

"I never get tired of hearing that," Frederick said. "We'll have to dance later."

"Oh, what fun," Dolly said, her eyes twinkling.

"So Lou, I hear you and Seymour go way back," Frederick said.

"All the way to Brooklyn," Lou replied.

"It's funny—I've been in Hollywood so long I can hardly remember where I'm from anymore!" Frederick joked.

Everyone laughed.

"I hate to break up a good time, but I'd like to go see my daughter before the ceremony. I hope we'll talk more at the reception."

"Absolutely," Frederick agreed. "Let's all meet at the bar."

Lou laughed. "Count me in." He turned to Seymour and asked, "Where can I find Dee?"

"Upstairs, third door on the left. Rose is with her."

Lou knocked on the bedroom door and Dee called, "Come in." She stood before a mirror in an ivory satin gown with a sweetheart neckline, the bodice covered in antique lace, her hair in loose spiral curls, her lips shimmering pink. Rose was fixing the hem of her dress.

"Oh, wow," he said, placing his hand over his heart. "My little Deanna Banana is all grown up. You're the most beautiful bride."

"Thank you, Daddy," she replied, smiling brightly.

"I'll leave you two alone for a minute," Rose said.

Dee hugged her tightly. "I can never thank you and Seymour enough."

"It's a great joy for us to be a part of your special day," Rose said. "We don't have children of our own, but we've always felt like second parents to you."

"Me too. I feel so blessed to have you both."

Rose smiled and left the room, closing the door behind her.

When they were alone, Lou took Dee's hand. "I'm so proud of you, my brilliant girl."

"You're going to make me cry. I was hoping to at least wait until the ceremony for that," she said, sniffling and dabbing the corners of her eyes.

"At the risk of ruining your mascara, I have to tell you that your mother would be proud of you too. From the moment you were born, we talked about how we wanted you to find something in this world that lit you up inside, and we hoped you'd also find true and lasting love. Now you have both."

"Anything good I have in my life is because you taught me how to live. I love you so much, Dad," she said, embracing him.

"I love you too."

"I wish Mom were here."

"Me too." He pulled back and said, "But Dee, she is here."

"You mean in spirit?"

"No, I mean in *you*. It's something you can never really understand unless you're a parent, but the best part of you lives in your child. That's why whenever I see you, I see your mother."

She hugged him again. When they let go, Lou said, "I spent some time with Rye outside."

"Is he nervous?" she asked.

He shook his head. "Not in the least. He's over the moon."

"I love him so much, Daddy."

"He feels the same about you. I knew it the second I saw you two together. I don't want to ruin any surprises, but he got you a very special wedding gift. It made me see just how deep his love runs."

She smiled. "That's sweet, but you know I don't care about material things."

"I do. He knows that too. You will care about this. This is a man who will never hurt you, only love you."

"I can't wait to marry him."

"He's waiting for you," Lou said. "Are you ready?"

She picked up her small bouquet of poppies and locked her arm in his. "I've never been more ready for anything in my life."

Rose instructed the string quartet to play and quickly took her seat up front. Dee and Lou stood at the end of the aisle. Rye smiled from ear to ear when he saw Dee for the first time, his eyes glistening at the sight of his bride-to-be. Everyone stood and turned to watch as they walked down the aisle, Dee's eyes glued to Rye. When they reached the wedding canopy, Lou kissed his daughter's cheek and said, "I love you. Be happy." He shook Rye's hand and claimed his seat in the front row. Rose held Dee's bouquet, and everyone sat down. Rye took both of Dee's hands in his and whispered, "You're stunning."

They stared into each other's eyes during the entire ceremony. Although they opted out of most traditions, they wanted their celebration to be filled with art, so Troy and Billy each read a poem they selected to mark the occasion. When it was time to recite their vows, Rye went first.

"Dee, I'm completely in love with you. I've made some mistakes in my life and people have called me rebellious, but you can trust that I will never be careless with your heart. From the night we met, you made me want to be an extraordinary man who is worthy of your great love. Now I want us to have everything—passionate love, passion for each other's work, and the joys of family. Dee, *you* are my extraordinary life. You are my home. I love you with all my heart, and I promise that I always will."

She sniffled and let go of his hands to delicately wipe her eyes. She took his hands again, and they smiled at each other. "Rye, I'm completely in love with you. Maybe the fact that we both knew heartache so early in our lives has made us appreciate beauty even more. The closeness we share is something I've never felt before. It's sacred. When we're together, I feel like I'm somehow more myself, and I want to spend my life making you feel the same way. I love you with all my heart and soul. I promise that I always will."

They were both smiling through their tears. Rye gently wiped away Dee's tears, and she did the same for him. She glanced back and saw her father, Seymour, and Rose all crying. Soon they were pronounced husband and wife. Rye took Dee's face in both of his hands, and they kissed passionately to huge applause. They held hands, smiling and giggling as they floated down the aisle as a married couple, their friends all on their feet clapping and tossing birdseed.

The quartet continued to play during cocktail hour as waitstaff passed plated hors d'oeuvres: smoked salmon crostini, blinis with caviar, savory rosemary palmiers, roasted figs with goat cheese, and mini lamb chops. Guests offered their congratulations to the happy couple. Dee introduced one of her friends as "Charlie, a talented street artist." After he walked away, Rye asked, "What kind of street art does he make?"

"Oh, you'd know it."

"He's not . . . Green? *The* Green?"

Dee nodded and said, "Shh, his identity is secret. Besides, I hadn't a clue who he was when we first met. Didn't matter to me. Talent is talent. Courage is courage."

Rye laughed. "You really are something."

At the photographer's request, they posed for photographs, including some with their fathers and hosts. Although Rye harbored negative feelings toward the entertainment press, they had decided to release one photo to the media in order to take the price off their heads. When they wrapped up the photo shoot, Rye whispered to Dee, "I need a few minutes alone with my amazing wife."

She touched his face and said, "There's nothing I want more than time alone with my handsome husband."

"Sweetheart, I got you a wedding present. Come into the house so I can give it to you in private." He took her hand and they walked inside.

"I got you a little something too. Let me run upstairs to get it," she said.

He waited at the bottom of the staircase, and when she returned, he led her to Seymour's home screening room. He held both of her hands in his. "You told me that you lost your mother's voice. I spoke to your father, and it turns out that Seymour, being the film enthusiast he is, made home movies of your parents on a camcorder when you were a little girl. Your father said you used to run away from the camera because you were so shy, so that's probably why you don't remember. Seymour went digging through his warehouse." He stopped and kissed her hands. "Sweetheart, he found the videos. We had them transferred onto a disc. I gave your father a copy too."

Her eyes became misty, her lips quivering. He squeezed her hands and said, "Just sit here."

She sat down, a bit stunned, and he darted to the back of the room. He turned the lights off, hit play, and then took the seat beside her, handing her a preemptive tissue. Suddenly, Lisette Schwartz was on the screen, talking and laughing, as radiant as a movie star.

"Oh my God," Dee gasped as her eyes flooded with hot tears. A moment later, Lisette twirled little Dee around. She couldn't have been more than five years old. Dee tried to run behind her mother, shy in front of the camera. Lisette laughed and said, "My sweet little Deanna." She scooped her up in her arms. "I love you, sweet girl."

When the video ended, Dee looked at Rye through a film of hot tears. He gently brushed away the salty water and pressed his forehead to hers. When she was able to speak again, she softly said, "You gave me my mother's voice."

"Seymour helped," he replied.

"You gave me my mother's voice. I love you more than I could ever say."

He kissed her softly. "I love you with all my heart. Forever."

She pulled back and used the tissue to dab her face. "Here," she said, handing him a small package wrapped in white paper and a red silk ribbon.

He opened it and discovered another disc. He looked at her quizzically.

"You told me you know your mother mostly from her films. I asked Seymour if there might be any footage you haven't seen. He had his assistant comb through the studio archives. Rye, they found tons of outtakes, things shot when they weren't officially rolling, even your mother in her dressing room. We pieced it together. There's one part at the end with dozens of shots just of her smiling, edited all together. Just like the end of *Cinema Paradiso*, only with smiling instead of kissing, because you told me how special her smile was."

He started to cry, unable to stop the steady stream of tears down his cheeks. She gently caressed the side of his face. "Thank you," he mumbled. "I don't know what's more special: that I have this incredible gift, or that you would think to do the same thing for me."

She smiled and whispered, "We know each other." She ran her finger along his temple. "I had help too. Seymour must have had a good chuckle, knowing we had both asked for the same thing."

"I can't believe he was able to do this," Rye said.

"He really is the great and powerful Wizard of Oz."

Soon, guests were escorted to the reception tent. Round tables were covered in white linens sprinkled with golden sparkles, gold dishes and flatware, bouquets of poppies, and hundreds of glowing white votive candles. Twinkling lights snaked across the ceiling of the tent, framing the dance floor while a full jazz band roared. The bride and groom took the first spin on the dance floor, their first as husband and wife. Rye held Dee's hand and placed his other hand on the small of her back. They twirled around, smiling at each other, their bodies pressed close together. The rest of the room fell away as they spun together among the sparkly lights. When the song ended, Rye walked Dee over to Lou for their dance. Lou couldn't stop grinning from ear to ear. "He gave me my present," Dee said. "It was like magic. I have her voice back. My heart is so full I don't know how to hold all the love." He kissed her forehead and they continued to dance.

Dee and Rye sat with their friends for dinner. When everyone was seated, waitstaff passed around flutes of Dom Perignon and Pellegrino. The singer called Lou up to the microphone.

Rye slung his arm around Dee, and she settled against his body.

"Good evening, everyone," Lou began. "I'm Lou Schwartz, Dee's father, and I couldn't be happier to be here celebrating this joyous occasion with all of you. I would like to thank Seymour and Rose for their incredible generosity opening up their home and hosting this special wedding celebration." Everyone clapped. "I've had the chance to get to know Rye's father Frederick tonight." Frederick held up his glass and nodded. "I know that I speak for us both and on behalf of Rebecca and Lisette when I say that all any parent dreams for their child is that they will find passion in their lives, and that they will know the joy of true, unconditional love. Tonight, our dreams have been fulfilled. Dee, you are a magnificent woman. I'm honored to be your father, and I am so proud of you. Rye, you are a wonderful man, and I'm thrilled that you and Dee found each other. Aspire to greatness in life and love, and never forget who you are. The world is yours. May you have every happiness. Cheers," he said, raising his flute.

"Cheers," everyone said, raising their glasses.

Dee blew her father a kiss. She sniffled and turned to Rye. They kissed and sipped their champagne.

Waitstaff descended on each table, taking orders and refilling flutes. The lavish meal began with a choice of a mesclun salad in a champagne vinaigrette, white asparagus soup, spicy tuna sushi and salmon sashimi, or beef carpaccio with shaved black truffles. The second course offered a choice of baked pumpkin, grilled Maine lobster, roast duck in a raspberry sauce, or chateaubriand. Dee held up her fork and said, "Honey, you have to try the pumpkin. It's heavenly."

Rye took the bite. "Mmm, that's good. Here, try this," he said, offering her a bite of lobster.

"Okay, you two are just too cute, feeding each other and all," Troy said. "But jeez, save something for the honeymoon."

Dee giggled.

"You never told us, where are you guys going?" Grey asked.

"I offered to take Dee to Hawaii or Paris or anywhere in the world," Rye said, "but she would rather stay here, so we're going to spend a week at her beach house."

"Paris would be lovely, but we just got back from Montana and soon we head out with Rye's band for their debut tour. We'll be traveling nonstop around Europe and the States for two months. I thought it would be nice to just stay put and relax," Dee explained.

"But don't think of dropping by," Rye joked. "We want to be alone."

They all laughed.

"Honestly, I can't think of anything better than lounging on the beach with my new husband," Dee said.

Rye leaned over and kissed her lightly.

"I've somehow become the cheapest date ever. Our first date was takeout from a drive-through, and our honeymoon is at Dee's own house," Rye said. "But I did hire a private chef to come and prepare dinner each night."

"I think that sounds perfect," Sara replied. Just then, she noticed a man staring at her from the next table. They had been making eyes at each other throughout the evening. Dee watched as Sara looked at the man and then bashfully turned away.

"Sara, that's Porter Lewis. He's a music producer," Dee said.

"Oh, uh, I wasn't . . ."

"You two have been looking at each other all night," Dee said.

Sara blushed. "He looks like he's older than me. And he's not my type."

Dee smiled. "He's in his early sixties, but he's young at heart. He's a fantastic musician and part owner of a music label."

"I'm not looking to meet anyone," she replied.

"That's the *best* time to meet someone," Dee insisted, discreetly nudging Rye.

"Hey, Porter!" Rye called, waving his hand. "Come on over for a minute."

Sara looked like she wanted to crawl under the table.

Porter had taken his suit jacket off and rolled up his sleeves, revealing his tattooed arms. He walked over and Rye said, "I wanted to see if you've met everyone. I'm sure you know Grey and Sloane. This is Troy; he's a comic book artist. And this is Sara; she's a film studies professor at UCLA."

"Very pleased to meet you," he said in his slight Southern drawl. He was focused only on Sara.

"Likewise," Sara replied.

"I must confess, I've been watching you all night. Would you like to dance?" he asked.

"Uh, well, sure," she said, standing up. He took her hand and led her to the dance floor.

"Bravo, Rye!" Troy said, raising his glass. "I didn't think it could be done. If anyone needs a spin around the dance floor with someone who colors outside the lines, it's Sara." They all peeked at the dance floor to see Sara and Porter smiling brightly and laughing, their connection palpable. Troy turned to Dee. "Maybe next time we all have brunch, we'll get to hear about something more interesting than her latest department meeting."

"Here's hoping," Dee said.

Everyone laughed.

When it was time to cut the cake, they first posed for photos with the five-tier red velvet confection covered in white icing, gold leaf trim, and edible red flowers.

Rye picked up a piece in his hands and fed Dee a small bite.

"It's delicious," she said.

"Oh, yeah," he said, and he leaned in and kissed her passionately. Everyone cheered. She giggled and picked up a small piece to feed him. He took a bite and smiled as everyone clapped.

Dee leaned in close and whispered, "My 'something blue' is a lacy blue garter. You'll have to take it off in private later."

"Let's get out of here," he joked.

She laughed. "After we have cake with our guests. But I promise I'll stay up all night making love with you."

"And every day after that?" he asked.

"Every day."

16

THEY SPENT THEIR BLISSFUL HONEYMOON SPLASHING around in the ocean, curling up together to watch the sunset, and making love day and night. When the idyllic week was over, they returned home and Rye released his first album to a warm reception. Critics called the album "an impressive first effort" and branded Rye "authentic, multi-talented, and riveting." The band began their nearly sold-out tour of small venues across Europe. Although nervous at first, Rye discovered that he loved performing live. It allowed him a new way to engage with an audience he had never experienced before, and he enjoyed talking about the experience with his new bride. Each night before he went on, Dee sat with him backstage and offered words of encouragement, reminding him to "Let go and have fun." As they left each venue, Rye stopped to sign autographs and take photos with fans, some screaming, "Ryder!" and others hollering, "Bruce Jones!" which never bothered him.

Dee gave a series of lectures about art and science at leading universities along the way. When they were scheduled for the morning, Rye was able to go with her, enamored each time he heard her speak. Tour bus life, although tiring, suited them. Rye jammed with the band, writing many new songs for a potential sophomore album, and Dee worked on her poetry collection. Inspired by audience questions posed at some of her lectures, she came up with an idea for a research study and decided to seek collaborators and funding when they returned home. On their days off, the pair dined in romantic bistros, strolled around museums, and attended theater and symphony performances. Each time, Rye asked, "Did you enjoy it?" Dee always smiled and said, "Yes, my love."

When they returned home after the US leg of the wildly successful tour, they settled into married life. Rye began shooting his new television series, and as promised he had a more predictable schedule. Dee completed her poetry collection and began working on grant applications. Her new novella was released to commercial success, but as usual critics were divided. One review was titled, "Pornography or Art?" Although she made it a policy to never read reviews, she decided that one was her favorite based on the title alone. She and Troy had a good laugh over it. Troy regularly brought over new illustrations for the graphic novel adaptation, which they both enjoyed working on almost as much as they enjoyed gossiping about Sara, who was having a heated affair with Porter.

Dee and Rye spent their free time relaxing in their home, going out with friends, and discussing art and travel and life. When one of them felt especially sentimental, they cuddled on the couch and watched the videos of their mothers, always smiling through their tears. As they fell more in love each day, they made love every night and many mornings out of mutual passion and their growing desire to start a family.

17

"HI, SWEETHEART. SORRY I'M LATE," RYE HOLLERED AS he walked into the house. "We had to do about a million and two takes on one scene today."

"That's okay. I'm in here, honey," she called from the kitchen.

"Wow, what's all this?" he asked, noticing the table glowing with white and gold votive candles.

"I felt like making something special for you," she said.

He kissed her tenderly. "It smells great. I'm famished, can't remember when I ate last."

"Well, then, you're in luck. I made chicken with a fresh apricot glaze, crispy saffron rice, and sautéed greens."

"The first meal you ever made for me, that weekend at your beach house," he recalled with an irrepressible smile. "It's hard to believe that was less than a year ago. So much has changed."

She smiled. "I was feeling nostalgic. Pour yourself a drink and have a seat."

"I missed you today. I'm so glad it's the weekend so we can relax."

"I missed you too," she said.

"So, how was your day?" he asked as he fixed himself a whiskey on the rocks.

"My colleagues and I got that big National Science Foundation grant we applied for to study the psychological effects of consuming art," she replied. "I'm the principal investigator. The project should keep me busy for a while, supervising the research and then writing a series of articles or maybe even a new book."

"Oh, baby, that's fantastic!" he said, coming over and hugging her. "You should have called me. I would have taken you out. This deserves a major celebration."

She caressed his cheek. "Actually, we have something else to celebrate, and I wanted to do it in private." She paused, staring into his eyes, and said, "Rye, I love you so much."

"I love you too," he said, kissing her. "What is it, sweetheart?"

"I'm pregnant."

"*What*?" he asked, breaking out into a huge grin. "Really?"

"I've been so tired lately and my period is late, so I took a test this morning. I went to the doctor to confirm. It's early, only about four weeks."

He picked her up and twirled her around in the air. When he gently set her down, they were both smiling and giggling.

"Are you happy?" she asked.

"Happy doesn't begin to describe how I feel. Dee, this is the best news I've ever heard." He paused and ran his fingers gently down the side of her face, his eyes becoming misty. "I love you with all my heart, and I'm so excited about this next chapter," he said, and he placed his hand on her tummy.

"Gee, we're late for our reservation. I hope Billy and Susan don't mind," Dee said.

"We're almost there," Rye replied, turning onto the next street. He picked up her hand and kissed it softly. "I'm sorry, it was my fault; I just had to have you. It was hard to tear myself out of bed."

"Being pregnant has its advantages. The hormones are wild. The only things I ever want to do are make love with you and sleep."

"I'm not complaining," he said with a chuckle. "Seriously, though, you've been so tired lately, for months now. Maybe we should have stayed in. To be honest, I'm getting a little worried about you."

"My doctor said it's fine. This extreme fatigue happens to some women. I just finished my first trimester, so maybe I'll start to have more energy."

"So long as those hormones keep up," he jested.

She giggled. "Yeah, when I told Sara and Troy about the baby at lunch today, I made the mistake of mentioning my, uh, my . . ."

"Insatiable desire for your handsome husband?"

She giggled. "Something like that. Naturally, Troy wanted to know all about our sexcapades. You know how he is. Sara immediately redirected the conversation to babyproofing the house."

"I can picture the whole thing."

"Oh, but Rye, you should have heard my father on the phone. He's bonkers, over-the-moon happy. Being a grandfather is something he's always hoped for. I told him that we're only telling a few people and asked him to keep it quiet, but I bet you anything the Brooklyn Eight has already heard the news, if not his whole community. He was just too excited."

"That's sweet. My father was happy for us too, in his way, where a minute later he was talking about the movie he's filming and the thirty-year-old he's screwing."

She laughed. "Rye, I'd like my dad to come for a visit soon, while I'm still able to get around normally. Then, after the baby is born, I was hoping he could stay with us for a while."

"Of course, sweetheart."

"After we tell Billy and Susan, let's not tell anyone else for a while. I know the doctor said we've made it through the riskiest time, but . . ."

"You're still nervous."

"Cautious. Life can never be taken for granted." She paused before continuing, "I've been thinking about my mother a lot lately."

"That's natural. I've been thinking about my mother too."

She reached over and placed her hand on his. "I know it's hard for you."

"I've actually been thinking about how my dad must have felt when she was killed. Even though they had problems in their marriage, I can imagine what it felt like for him, not being able to protect the mother of his child. Now that we're having a baby, I think I can begin to understand. It's hard to explain. Maybe it's different for women." He paused and glanced at her. "I've never wanted to protect anyone the way I do now with you, and our baby. It's like the moment I found out you were pregnant, some instinct kicked in that I've never felt before."

"I love you," she said.

"I love you too," he replied as he parked the car.

"That's hysterical," Billy said as they all stepped outside, talking and laughing after a wonderful dinner.

Susan hugged Dee and said, "That was fun."

"It was," Dee replied, unable to contain a yawn. "Oh, gee. I'm sorry."

"Don't be," Susan said. "I've been there. We're so excited for you guys."

"Couldn't be happier," Billy added. He shook Rye's hand. "From the day you told me about Dee, I knew she was the one and that everything would change. Congratulations, old friend."

"So, we'll see you guys again in about a week at the Globes," Rye said.

Just then, a few paparazzi appeared out of nowhere, screaming their names and frantically taking photographs.

Billy and Rye smiled at the photographers, allowing them their shot. Rye grabbed Dee's hand and they tried to walk toward their car, but one photographer who regularly contributed to *Celebs in the Wild* stepped directly in front of them, furiously snapping pictures.

"I can't see," Dee said, blinded by the flashes.

"Hey, come on, man. You got your pictures," Rye said, trying to shield Dee.

But the photographer wouldn't relent. "Let's see Bruce Jones in action," he hollered. "Where's that famous temper of yours, Ryder? You been drinking? Give me something good."

"I'm not that guy anymore. I'm just trying to get my wife home. Have a good night, buddy." Rye tried to maneuver past him, but the photographer wouldn't step out of their path.

Dee put her arm in front of her eyes. "It's blinding. I'm afraid I'm going to fall," she said.

"That's it, asshole," Rye said, lunging at him and pushing him to the ground. His camera cracked on the concrete. Rye turned to Dee and put his hands on her shoulders. "You okay, sweetheart?"

"Someone call the cops!" the photographer hollered. "That's assault!"

"You assaulted us, asshole!" Rye screamed.

Pedestrians on both sides of the street stopped to watch the commotion, whipping out their cell phones to record the incident.

"I got it on film. You won't get away with this," the photographer said, picking up his broken camera and slowly rising to his feet with a self-satisfied smile.

The maître d' came running out of the restaurant. "What's going on?" he asked.

"Ryder Field just assaulted me on camera and in front of witnesses. Call the police or I'll sue you for allowing this to happen on your property."

"He harassed us!" Rye groaned.

"I'm so sorry, Mr. Field. Please wait here while I call the authorities. I'm sure we can get this straightened out in no time."

"This is fucking bullshit," Rye grumbled.

"Honey," Dee said, rubbing his arm. "Please calm down. Don't make it worse. That's what he wants. He's setting you up."

"Billy, please take Dee home," Rye said.

"No, I'm staying with you," Dee protested.

"Please, Dee. I just want you safe at home so I don't have to worry. It will only make things worse if you stay."

"I don't want to leave you. Plus, I'm a witness. I can tell the police what happened. He was practically on top of us. He assaulted us."

"It's all been recorded. Please, sweetheart, just go with Billy and call my lawyer." He brushed her hair out of her face. "Don't worry. It'll be fine."

"Come on, Dee. We'll get you home," Billy said, reaching for her hand.

Three hours later, Rye wandered into their bedroom and found Dee sitting in bed waiting for him.

He sat on the edge of the bed beside her. "Oh, honey," she said, throwing her arms around him. "Are you okay?"

He hugged her tightly. "They charged me with assault and battery. Don't worry. Larry bailed me out, and he's already working on getting the charges dropped. We're going to pay this lowlife off. It kills me to give him money, but it's the fastest way to make it go away. It'll be done by morning." He looked at her, brushed the hair from her face, and said, "I'm so sorry, sweetheart. I never should have let this happen. It'll be on every magazine cover, trashy website, and tabloid TV show."

"Rye, that guy baited you. It was so obviously a setup. You were protecting me. They should have arrested *him*."

"I just hate these assholes so much, after . . ."

"After what they did to your mother. I know, honey."

"I couldn't bear anyone exploiting or hurting you or our baby. I love you both so much." He rested his hand on her stomach and asked, "Are you okay? Tell me the truth."

She nodded. "I'm fine, really I am. All I want is to hold you. Take your clothes off and crawl into bed. Just put it out of your mind. No one can hurt us. We're together and we love each other. Nothing else matters."

18

DEE STEPPED OUT OF THE BATHROOM IN A FLOWING pale-pink chiffon gown adorned in rosettes, her hair in long spiral curls, her lips stained pink.

Rye gasped when he saw her. "Oh, sweetheart. You're stunning. You positively glow."

"You look so handsome," she said, straightening his tuxedo tie and adjusting his collar. "Do you think it covers my tummy?" she asked. "I'm not ready for the whole world to know we're expecting."

He put one hand on her belly and the other on her cheek. "No one will know. God, you are so beautiful. You've made me the happiest man in the world."

She kissed him softly.

"Sweetheart, I know how tired you've been. Are you sure you're feeling up to this? It's just a stupid awards show; you don't have to come."

"The love of my life was nominated for a Golden Globe. I wouldn't miss this night for anything."

"I know you think awards are silly," he said.

"Honey, I'm so proud of you. You're an amazing actor. It was a gorgeous performance. Let's go celebrate."

"Shall we?" he asked.

She hooked her arm through his, and they headed out to the waiting limo.

—

They strolled hand in hand down the bustling red carpet through a frenzy of flashbulbs as fans and press screamed, "Ryder, over here!" Each time he stopped to speak with someone, he gave Dee's waist a gentle squeeze and pecked her cheek. Never one for the spotlight, she stood back shyly, smiling politely at reporters. One entertainment show reporter called Rye over for a quick interview.

"We're standing here with Ryder Field, nominated tonight in the Best Supporting Actor category. Ryder, how do you feel about your nomination?"

"It's very flattering," Rye said. He smiled, glanced back at Dee, and continued, "But my wife always reminds me that the work is what really matters. It's about making good art, not receiving awards. Tonight, I'm just glad to be here celebrating with my colleagues and friends."

Dee blushed.

"Audiences still know you best from your starring role on *The Mission*. You've recently returned to the small screen to high ratings and the delight of your fans. How do you feel being back on television?"

"I'm loving it. I'm especially grateful that we're able to shoot right here in LA."

"Thank you for your time, and good luck tonight, Ryder."

"Thank you," Rye replied.

He put his arm around Dee and pecked her cheek again, and they continued down the red carpet. They finally reached the star-studded ballroom filled with joyful chatter. The room was adorned with massive chandeliers, endless ribbons of crystal balls, and round tables lavishly set in white and gold. As Dee looked around the room, Seymour and Rose spotted them and waved them over.

"Dee, you look radiant tonight," Seymour said, hugging her. "Pregnant women always shine."

She opened her mouth in surprise and he quickly said, "Your father told me. Don't worry, we know you're keeping it quiet for now." He paused, looking at her affectionately. "You remind me so much of your mother," he added, squeezing her wrists. "She was never more beautiful than when she was carrying you."

She smiled. "Thank you, Seymour. We were planning to tell you."

"Lou is so excited to become a grandfather. I've never heard him happier about anything," Seymour said.

"You and Rose will also be grandparents to our baby."

"We can't wait," Rose said.

They continued talking for a while before excusing themselves to catch up with some of Rye's friends and colleagues. Soon they took their seats alongside Billy and Susan. Waitstaff served a cold strawberry soup with a cucumber and pomegranate garnish, the first of an extravagant three-course vegan meal, although everyone at the table opted to chat, not eat. Soon the ceremony began.

During the opening monologue, the host called out several celebrities. At one point, the camera panned to Rye and the host said, "Perhaps one of the biggest surprises this year is that Ryder Field, the consummate bachelor known for being a bit of a renegade, has tied the knot. That's right, ladies, he's taken. But as last week's tabloids reminded us, he's still got that rebellious streak. We all wish his wife well." Rye laughed and draped his arm around Dee. She looked down, giggling.

Rye's category, Best Supporting Actor in a Motion Picture, was the second award of the evening. Sloane Hewson presented the award, ripping open the envelope and announcing, "And the Golden Globe goes to . . . Ryder Field!" Rye smiled brightly and turned to Dee, kissing her lovingly as the audience applauded.

"Congratulations, honey," she whispered, her hand on his face.

Billy gave him a fist bump and said, "Good job, buddy."

Rye made his way to the stage, where Sloane pecked his cheek and handed him the coveted golden trophy.

"Thank you to the Hollywood Foreign Press for this tremendous honor. I want to thank everyone who worked on this film, the entire cast and crew; it was a great privilege to share this experience with you." Then he looked straight at Dee and said, "Finally, I would like to thank my brilliant wife. Dee, I love you with all my heart. You make this life extraordinary. Thank you for making me the luckiest guy in the world."

Her eyes glossed over with tears as she smiled bashfully at him. He waved to the crowd and headed offstage with his trophy. Backstage, Rye did the press circuit before returning to their table half an hour later. He sat down, everyone at his table quietly congratulating him. He took Dee's hand, kissed it softly, and smiled at her. She leaned over and whispered in his ear, "I love you so much. You're such a beautiful artist. I'm so proud of you, and not just tonight."

"That means everything coming from you. How are you feeling, sweetheart?" he asked.

"I'm tired. My energy is just so low."

"Let's get out of here. We don't need to stay for the whole thing. People will understand."

"It's your big night. You need to stay, support the film, celebrate with your colleagues. But if you don't mind, maybe I'll have the driver take me home and I can send him back for you later."

"Sweetheart, are you sure? I can go with you."

She stroked his face. "Enjoy this special night. Stay until the fat lady sings, and then go to the after-parties. I'll be sound asleep as soon as my head hits the pillow." Then she gave him a sultry look and whispered, "But if you want a private celebration when you get home, wake me."

He kissed her lightly. "I won't be late."

She smiled and rubbed the tip of her nose against the tip of his. Rye watched adoringly as she left, gliding across the room like a princess.

When the ceremony ended, everyone mingled, making plans to head to the after-parties.

"Are you sure you don't want to join us for a while?" Billy asked Rye. "Never known you to pass up a celebratory drink. You don't have to stay all night."

"I should really get home to Dee," he replied.

"Was she feeling alright?" Susan asked. "Has she been nauseated?"

He shook his head. "No, but she's exhausted all the time."

"I was the same way when I was pregnant," Susan said. "She'll probably be asleep; come hang out and celebrate."

"Thanks. You guys have fun. I'm gonna head home to check on her. It'll be a zoo getting out of here, and I told her I wouldn't be late."

"Congrats, buddy," Billy said, hugging him.

"Good night, guys," Rye said, and he headed out.

Hungry at the end of a long night, Rye had the driver stop at a drive-through to pick up a burger on the way home. When the driver dropped him off, he wandered up to the door, his golden statuette in one hand and a takeout bag in the other. "What the fuck?" he mumbled, alarmed when he saw that the front door was ajar. He stepped inside and put the award and takeout on the entry table, immediately noticing a framed photograph of his mother was turned over. A cold shiver ran up his spine as he sprinted upstairs to his bedroom and flung the door open. The bed was still made. He started running through the house, looking in every room, hysterically screaming, "Dee! Dee!"

She was nowhere to be found.

Part Three

19

"MR. FIELD, WE NEED YOU TO CALM DOWN," OFFICER Smith said as the other police officers roamed around the house.

"My pregnant wife is missing," Rye said, clutching his head. "Please, you have to find her."

"Like I said, we've filed a missing person's report, although it's early to assume the worst," Officer Smith replied. "There are no signs of forced entry, and nothing seems to be disturbed."

"But the photograph . . ." Rye started.

"Yes, you mentioned the photograph several times."

"Listen, my wife is smart. I think she did that as a sign to me. You need to do something," Rye pleaded. "Do you know who I am? Who my family is?"

"Yes, we do, Mr. Field."

"Then you know what happened to my mother, Rebecca Field."

"I sure do. Just awful. I wasn't with the force back then, but we all still feel it, that she wasn't found in time. It's a dark shadow over this town."

"Please don't let my wife suffer the same fate. Something terrible has happened to her. You need to do everything you can to find her."

Just then, Larry Wentworth, Rye's attorney, walked in. "Rye, how are you holding up?" he asked, giving him a pat on the back.

"I'm a wreck," Rye replied, starting to sob. "Thank you for coming."

"Who are you?" Officer Smith asked.

"Larry Wentworth, attorney," he said, handing the officer his business card.

"What made you call your lawyer?" Officer Smith asked with a raised eyebrow.

"I thought maybe he could help. I'm grasping at straws here," Rye whimpered.

"Let's just go over all the facts again," Officer Smith said.

"Yeah, okay," Rye muttered, barely able to get the words out.

"You and your wife went to the Golden Globes. She was tired and decided to leave early, after you won your category. You didn't think you should go with her?"

"She told me to stay, she insisted. She was just going home to go to sleep, and she wanted me to enjoy the night. That's how she is, always thinking of others."

"Then, when the ceremony was over, you decided to skip the after-parties because you wanted to check on her, yet you stopped to get takeout. Why would you do that if you were concerned about your wife?"

"I hadn't eaten all night. I thought she'd be home asleep. I wasn't concerned at the time; I just wanted to be with her. I love Dee, and I'd rather be here with her than at some dumb party."

"Is it possible she went to a friend's house?"

"No. She would never do that without telling me, nor would she leave her purse, keys, and cell phone. She said she was going home to sleep. I've called all her local friends, and no one's heard from her. I've given you their names; you can check for yourself."

"What about her family?" Officer Smith asked.

"Her father lives in Florida. I haven't called him yet because I don't want to worry him."

"So, you come home and your wife is missing. You call the police and your lawyer, but not her father," Officer Smith said with an air of suspicion.

"It's the middle of the night on the East Coast. I didn't want to call and worry him until we knew more. She's everything to him."

"Uh-huh," Officer Smith replied coldly. "Mr. Field, have you and your wife been having problems? Any recent arguments?"

"What?" Rye bellowed.

"Calm down, Rye," Larry said, patting his arm. He turned to the officer and asked, "Is my client under suspicion here?"

"I'm just trying to get the facts," Officer Smith replied.

"First you tell me it's early to file a missing person's report, and now you're insinuating I had something to do with my wife's disappearance?" Rye asked.

"When a woman goes missing, her spouse is often involved. We can't rule it out. Pregnancy can be a difficult time for many relationships. Hormones. Jealousy. Were you having problems?"

"Don't answer that," Larry said.

Rye ignored the advice and replied, "I love my wife more than anything in the world. We've been over the moon about the baby. No, we weren't having any problems. Please, you need to start looking for her."

"Mr. Field, have you ever assaulted your wife? Could she be afraid of you?"

"How can you ask me that?" Rye said, almost hysterical.

"You've been arrested for assault and battery twice, most recently only about a week ago. I saw the photographs. You looked enraged. Maybe your temper got out of control again tonight. If there's something you need to tell us . . ."

"Don't answer that," Larry repeated.

Ignoring his lawyer again, Rye said, "Those so-called assaults were with the paparazzi who were hassling me to provoke a response. The most recent incident happened when a photographer was harassing Dee. She's pregnant and I was trying to protect her. It was a setup to get high-value photos of me and then shake me down for a payout. The charges were dropped."

"Do you have a prenuptial agreement?"

"My God, you have some nerve," Rye grumbled. "You're not listening to me."

"Please just answer the question."

"No," Rye said.

"That could make a divorce very expensive."

"My wife has money of her own."

"It's common knowledge that you have a net worth of around one hundred million dollars. Is your wife that wealthy?"

"No. But this is all irrelevant. My wife and I are not getting divorced. We are not having any problems. We don't even argue about what movie to watch on a Friday night. We're making a family together. It's been the happiest time in our lives."

"Can anyone vouch for your whereabouts tonight?"

"Yeah, the thousands of people at the Globes tonight and the millions who watched it on TV. The driver can confirm when he picked me up and dropped me off. When he was driving me home, he told me he'd driven my wife earlier and that he watched her get safely inside the house. He said," he began, his voice starting to crack, "he said she talked about how proud she was of me. Go talk to him." He ran his hand through his hair. "You're wasting time."

"I'm sorry, Mr. Field. I'm required to cover all the bases."

Just then, another officer came downstairs. He whispered something to Officer Smith, who whispered something in return.

"Mr. Field, my colleague noticed the safe in your bedroom closet was ajar. It's empty. Is it normally empty?" Officer Smith asked.

"No, we keep cash in there. It must have been a burglary. Dee must have walked in on it. Oh my God!" he cried, gripping his head with his hands.

"Mr. Field, there's no sign of forced entry, and I presume your wife had access to the safe," Officer Smith said. "There's nothing to be embarrassed about. Is it possible your wife left you?"

"You're not listening to me. Dee and I are madly in love. We're expecting a baby. She would never leave me," he said, frustration reverberating from every syllable.

"Do you own any other properties where she could be?"

"Dee had a house in Malibu that we held on to after we got married. We use it on weekends and holidays sometimes. But she would never go there without telling me."

"Here," Officer Smith said, handing him a small notepad and pen. "Write down the address and I'll send someone over to check it out."

Rye wrote down the address and handed the pad back to the officer. He looked him directly in the eyes and said, "My mother was murdered by a crazed fan after going home early from an awards show." He paused, breaking down into tears. Larry rubbed his back. Rye took a deep, steadying breath and continued, "This is my worst fear. I love my wife. I love my wife more than anything in the world. Please find her."

"I'm going to call the station. Why don't you go change into something more comfortable? I think it's going to be a long night."

"Come on, Rye," Larry said. "Let's get you out of this tux. I'll go upstairs with you."

"Yeah, alright," he mumbled.

A little while later, Rye came back downstairs wearing jeans and a gray pullover. "Mr. Field, there's been a development," Officer Smith said. "There's no one at your beach house, and we've confirmed your whereabouts throughout the evening. I had a couple of my guys canvass the area, and one of them found this about a block down the road," he continued, holding up a light pink rosette in a clear evidence bag. "We believe this came from your wife's dress."

"Oh my God," Rye said, looking at the small piece of fabric. "Yes, yes," he mumbled through tears. "That's from her gown."

The officer sighed. "I'm so sorry, but we now believe your wife has been abducted. I've alerted the FBI. They're on their way."

20

"Can you confirm that my client is no longer under suspicion?" Larry asked the federal agent.

"We're not prepared to rule anything out, but he's not the focus of our investigation at this time." The agent turned his attention to Rye and said, "Mr. Field, we spoke with your wife's father, and he was adamant that we direct our energy elsewhere. Apparently, Mrs. Field called him on her way home tonight, gushing about how happy she is. We also spoke with her close friends, and they confirmed that you seemed happily married. No one who knows her believes you had anything to do with her disappearance. They all independently said you are the love of her life."

Rye's eyes teared. "And she's the love of mine." He paused and asked, "You don't think this was a random burglary, do you?"

"Let's take a seat in the living room," the agent replied as the army of FBI agents and police officers milled around the house. Rye and Larry led the way and sat together on the couch; the agent sat in a chair opposite them. "At this point, we can't rule anything out. Given the undisturbed nature of the scene, the disabled surveillance camera outside the front door, your celebrity status, and the parallels to your mother's infamous abduction, we believe this was likely a targeted crime."

"My God," Rye muttered, running his hands through his hair. He mumbled to himself, barely audible, "I can't lose her. I can't . . ."

"Mr. Field, our best chance of finding your wife unharmed is if this is part of a ransom plan. We're set up to run traces on your cell phone and the landline, and we'll record any incoming calls. If no demand is made, we may have to turn to the media and involve the public to help locate her."

Rye gripped his head with his hands, the distress on his face worsening.

"We're not there yet. My gut still tells me we're in for a ransom demand," the agent explained. "In the meantime, it would help if we could identify any possible suspects."

"Yeah, I understand," Rye said.

"Who has access to the house?" the agent asked.

"The cleaning woman has a key and her own security code for the alarm. I already gave her contact information to the police."

"They checked her out. No one else has access? A gardener, an assistant, family members?"

He shook his head.

"Does your wife have any enemies?" the agent asked.

"No. Dee's the sweetest person I've ever met. Everyone loves her."

"Has she been hassled by anyone lately?"

"Not that I'm aware of."

"What about ex-boyfriends?"

"She dated a man named Russell Winthrop for a couple of years shortly before we met, but to my knowledge, they've had no contact since. He's an investment banker in New York City."

"Did she ever mention any problems in their relationship? Was she afraid of him? Any jealousy, physical abuse, that kind of thing?"

"No, nothing like that. She only said good things about him. The only other ex-boyfriend I know about is a guy named Jett Reed. He's an artist. They dated about fifteen years ago, but he drifted in and out of her life after that. She told me he has substance abuse problems, and sometimes she'd bail him out of things."

"How so?"

"She gave him money a couple of times."

"Do you know when she saw him last?"

"He called her about six months ago. He moved to San Francisco and had come to LA for an art show. He invited her, but she didn't go."

"Any problems in their relationship? Violence?"

Rye shook his head. "I think they had problems because of his alcohol and drug use, but nothing violent. She cared about him. Her friends Sara and Troy would probably know more about her past relationships."

"Our agents have already spoken with them both. Let's shift gears. Have you been hassled by anyone lately? Anyone have a grudge against you?"

"A paparazzo provoked an argument with me a week ago, for a payout. We settled out of court and I think it's over, but I don't know if he has a grudge."

"You're a famous actor. What about fans?"

Rye broke down in choked sobs. He slumped over onto his lap, a puddle of tears. Larry patted his back, trying to comfort him. He sniffled, looked up, and wiped his nose with his sleeve. "I'm sorry, it's just that a fan murdered my mother. Now the thought that . . ." he trailed off, breaking down again.

"Mr. Field, I can only imagine how difficult this is for you, but time is of the essence. Are you aware of any threats from your fans? Maybe superfans, groupies, that kind of thing. Any people we should look into?"

He wiped his face and replied, "My fans have always been kind to me. Some of them are pretty intense, but I've never felt threatened. There are a bunch of fan websites for the really devoted, but I never look at that stuff. We can contact my management team and see what they know. Fan mail is sent to my agent." He turned to Larry. "Will you please take care of that?"

Larry nodded and excused himself to make the call. Just then, a police officer wandered into the room and said, "William Sumner is here. He's waiting in the foyer. Should we let him in?"

"He's one of my closest friends. I called him for support," Rye explained.

The agent gestured at the officer to let him in. Billy rushed into the room and Rye rose to greet him. "Oh, buddy, how are you holding up?" Billy asked, embracing him tightly.

"Not good," Rye said, starting to cry. "I can't believe this is happening. I love her so much. I can't lose her."

"I know, bud. They'll find her."

When they eventually parted, all the men sat down. The agent continued with his questioning. "Mr. Field, can you think of . . ." But before he could finish his sentence, the house telephone rang. They all went barreling into the kitchen.

Rye stood anxiously by the receiver, watching the FBI agents scrambling around. "Answer now," one said, nodding at Rye.

"Hello?"

"I have your wife," a man's voice replied.

Rye shuddered. "Please, don't hurt her. I'll do anything you want."

"The price for your wife's return is two million dollars cash."

"Let me talk to her so I know she's alright," Rye said.

"This isn't a negotiation. She's unharmed. If you want her to remain that way, get the money ready."

"How is this going to work?"

"I'll call you early tomorrow morning with instructions."

"How do I know . . ." The caller hung up before Rye could finish his sentence.

Everyone anxiously turned to the agent who was running the trace. He shook his head and said, "Burner phone. Untraceable."

The agent in charge asked, "Did you recognize the caller's voice?"

"No," he replied, shaking his head.

"I know it doesn't feel like it now, but this is good news. We have good reason to believe your wife is alive."

Rye started crying again. Billy rubbed his back and said, "They're going to get Dee back."

"She must be terrified. What if they've hurt her? She's pregnant," Rye wailed.

"Mr. Field, we're going to use every minute we have between now and when he calls back to try to determine the perp's identity and locate your wife. In the event that we're unsuccessful, we also need to prepare for the exchange. Can you secure the funds?"

"Yeah." He turned to Larry and said, "Get the money."

"Obviously, we'll try to nab the bastard without giving him a cent," the agent said.

"I don't care about the money. Just help me get my wife back." He paused for a moment and asked, "In ransom cases like this, what percentage of the victims make it out alive?"

The agent sighed. "It's best not to think about statistics. Let's just all concentrate on bringing Mrs. Field back home safely."

"Yeah, okay," Rye muttered, disheartened.

"Any news?" Rye asked the agent.

"Her exes checked out. Mr. Winthrop is in New York City with no knowledge of any of this. He was quite distressed and hopes we find her."

"What about Jett?" Rye asked.

"Mr. Reed is in a rehabilitation center in San Francisco. He's not in any condition to have orchestrated something like this. We've also scoured social media fan groups. Nothing."

Rye sighed.

Without any new leads, everyone became increasingly anxious after sunrise, huddling by the landline in the kitchen, waiting for the ransom call they all prayed would come.

"Here, buddy, let me top that off," Billy said, refilling Rye's coffee mug. "You sure you don't want to eat something?"

Rye put his head down on the table.

"They're gonna bring her home," Billy insisted. "Hey, look at me."

Rye lethargically lifted his head and looked at his friend through bloodshot eyes.

"This isn't what happened to your mother. History is not repeating. You and Dee, well . . . I just know you'll be together for a lifetime," Billy said.

"Remember when I met her? I was worried it would be hard to be married, to unselfishly think of someone else."

"I remember," Billy said.

"It hasn't been, not for a single minute. It's been the most natural thing in the world."

Just then, Rye's cell phone rang. He straightened up. An agent looked at him and said, "We're ready to run a trace, but we doubt it's him. He'll use the landline again. You can pick up."

"Hello?" Rye said.

"Hi, Rye," a woman's voice replied.

"Who is this?"

"It's me, Lucy. I know it's been a long time."

"Oh, uh, sorry, Luce," he said in a perplexed voice. "I can't talk. I'm dealing with something urgent."

"Rye, don't hang up. Your wife is with me."

"What?" Rye asked, his eyes wide.

All the agents and officers started gesturing at each other.

"Rye, I didn't mean for this to happen. Things . . ."

"What did you do?" Rye demanded, instantly enraged.

"Last night, when I knew you'd be at the Golden Globes, my boyfriend and I went to your place. I took a gamble that you didn't change the locks or security code. We were only planning to take the cash you leave in the safe. You owed it to me, Rye. What do you think it was like for me dating a famous actor and then being cast aside? We weren't married, and . . ."

"What the hell are you talking about? When we broke up, I gave you money to get on your feet. For Christ's sake, we dated, that doesn't mean I have to support you for the rest of your life. And it damn sure doesn't mean you can break into my house!"

"The money you gave me is long gone. It doesn't matter now. I need you to know I never intended for anyone to get hurt."

"What did you do to my wife?" he roared.

"She walked in on us. We thought you'd both be gone for hours. Then Derrek, my boyfriend, thought we should take her, you know, for the ransom money. It all spiraled out of control before I could stop it. But then after you agreed to pay the money . . ."

Rye took a deep breath and squeezed his eyelids shut. "What happened? Is Dee hurt?"

"She's fine. It's just . . . This morning, Derrek started talking crazy, saying how we couldn't let her go because she knows our identities. Rye, he has a gun."

"So help me God, if anything happens to her . . ."

"She's okay. I got scared, so I tricked Derrek into going into the shed out back. I clubbed him over the head and locked the door. You have to come right now. I don't think he can get out, but . . ."

"Where are you?" Rye demanded.

"I know the cops will be there, but you have to come inside alone. If I see anyone else coming up to the door, well, I have his gun and I'm not saying I'd use it, but . . ."

"Lucy, where are you?"

"In the house he rents in Los Feliz. I'll give you the address."

"Mr. Field, we can't allow you to do this. We can't be responsible for putting another civilian in harm's way. We will handle it," the agent insisted.

"Like you handled my mother's kidnapping? She was killed and you guys let the media get hold of the crime scene photos."

"Rye, maybe you should listen to them," Larry said.

"You all heard what Lucy said. If I go to the door alone, I think she'll let Dee go. I know Lucy. She won't hurt us."

"With all due respect, Mr. Field," the agent said, "you didn't think she was capable of this in the first place."

"Let me do this. Please. If you guys surround them and try to negotiate, or worse, storm the house, you could escalate things irreparably. Let's just do what Lucy said. I'll take my chances. We can't waste any more time debating this."

"We can't guarantee your safety."

"I'll sign a release or whatever you need from me. But if you don't let me do this and something happens to my wife, I'll sue the hell out of you."

The agent sighed and shrugged his shoulders defeatedly. "Meet us outside in two minutes. Just you. When we get to the scene, we'll get you in a bulletproof vest and put a listening device on you. That's the best we can do."

"Okay. Let's hurry."

Billy stopped Rye. "Buddy, this isn't a movie or television show. You're not Bruce Jones."

"Believe me, no one understands that better than I do. What would you do if this were Susan or your girls?"

Billy took a deep breath and asked, "Is there anything I can do to help?"

"Call her ob-gyn and ask her to meet us at the hospital. The number is on the refrigerator."

21

Rᴙᴇ ᴄᴀᴜᴛɪᴏᴜsʟʏ ᴀᴘᴘʀᴏᴀᴄʜᴇᴅ ᴛʜᴇ sᴍᴀʟʟ ʀᴀɴᴄʜ-style house. Before he could knock on the door, it swung open. He stepped inside and immediately saw Dee tied to a chair in the far corner, duct tape across her mouth. She was still wearing her evening gown, and mascara ran in streaks down her cheeks.

"Oh my God," he gasped, darting over to her. He knelt on the floor and gently pulled the tape from her mouth. She burst into tears. "It's okay, sweetheart. I'm here," he said, caressing her face. "I'm so sorry. I'm so sorry, Dee. You're safe," he assured her, frantically untying her. "Did they hurt you?"

She shook her head, crying hysterically, her whole body shaking. "The baby. I'm worried about the baby," she sputtered in between sobs.

"I'm gonna get you out of here."

The door slammed. He turned and saw Lucy, trembling with a look of shock in her eyes.

"How could you do this?" he screamed. "I could fucking kill you!"

"Rye, I'm sorry. Things got out of hand. I didn't mean for any of this to happen," she said.

"Where's the asshole who helped you?" Rye demanded.

"He's still locked in the shed," she replied. "I would never have let him hurt her."

He turned back to Dee. "Sweetheart, I'm going to get you to the hospital," he said, and he scooped her up in his muscular arms. She clung to him as he walked toward the door. He glared at Lucy and growled, "Open the fucking door."

"You have to understand. We were together for four years, and you said you never wanted to get married again. *Four years,* Rye. You married her after four months," Lucy said.

"Open the fucking door," he seethed.

She reluctantly opened the door, and Rye carried Dee to the waiting ambulance as police and FBI agents swarmed the house. He gently laid her down on a gurney as EMTs rushed to her side. A couple of federal agents approached them.

"We need to ask her some questions," one of the agents said.

"You'll have to wait. We're taking my wife to the hospital immediately," Rye said.

"We'll meet you there," the agent responded.

"Rye," Dee called. "Please don't leave me."

"I'm not going anywhere, sweetheart," he assured her, taking her hand.

"You can ride with us," an EMT said as they loaded her into the ambulance.

They sped off, sirens blazing as an EMT began taking her vitals. "Are you hurt?"

"No," she whimpered. "I'm fourteen weeks pregnant," she said, tears cascading down her face. "I need my husband."

"I'm right here, sweetheart," Rye said, caressing her forehead. "I'm right here. Just breathe. Just take slow breaths."

"Her vital signs are good," the EMT reported. "No obvious signs of injury."

When they arrived at the hospital, they were rushed into an exam room. A nurse helped Dee out of her ball gown and into a hospital gown. As the doctor examined her, she kept begging, "Please, I'm fine. I'm pregnant. Is my baby okay?"

"We need to check you first," he said.

She continued crying, and Rye stroked her hair and whispered calmly into her ear about how much he loved her and that she was safe.

"How is she?" Rye asked the doctor.

"Other than some minor bruising on her wrists and mild dehydration, which we'll take care of with an IV, she seems fine. Depending on what her obstetrician says, we may be able to release her in a few hours once she's hydrated." He turned to Dee and said, "You've been through an awfully traumatic ordeal, Mrs. Field. Would you like to speak to someone? I can get a psych consult. It might help."

"No, thank you, I'm fine. Please, I just want to know about our baby."

"We called ahead. Her ob-gyn should be here," Rye said.

"She's waiting for you in ultrasound. We'll take you both there now."

As Dee lay on the exam table in the imaging suite, each passing second feeling like an eternity, her doctor said, "Please lift your gown. I'm going to rub this jelly on your belly. It will feel a little cold."

Rye stood by her side, holding her hand and gently stroking her forehead. They stared into each other's eyes.

Her doctor placed the ultrasound wand on her belly and turned the monitor on. "Okay, I'm going to press on your belly; it will be uncomfortable but shouldn't hurt. Let's just try to get a good image," she said. They both turned toward the monitor, the air in the room thick with nervous anticipation and unspoken prayers. The doctor smiled brightly. "Your babies are just fine."

"Babies?" Dee asked.

"Congratulations, you're having twins! See?" she said, pointing to the screen. "Here's baby number one, and here's baby number two."

"Oh my God," Dee said, hot tears streaming down her face. She turned to Rye and saw that his eyes were flooded too. "What do you think?" she asked.

"It's the best news I've ever heard," he replied, leaning down and kissing her softly. "You were worried about having an only child. Now our babies will always have each other."

Suddenly, there was a beautiful chorus of thumping in the room. "And those are the heartbeats," the doctor said. "Strong and just as I'd want them to be at this stage."

Dee and Rye couldn't stop smiling and giggling through their happy tears.

"You're sure they're alright?" Dee asked.

"Yes, no doubt about it. This explains why you've been so tired; multiples can often cause fatigue early in pregnancy. Would you like to know the sex? It's a bit early, but we can give it a look."

Rye ran his finger down Dee's cheek. "It's up to you, sweetheart."

"Meeting you was the best thing that ever happened to me. It was the most glorious surprise of my life. Let's have another surprise, two of them."

He leaned down and kissed her forehead and then turned to the doctor and said, "Show them to us again, please. I want to see the faces of my children."

A little while later, Dee was propped up against pillows, resting in her hospital bed with an IV drip, clutching her sonogram of the twins. Rye came into the room and said, "I spoke with your father. He wanted to catch the first flight. It wasn't easy to convince him to stay put."

"I'd love for him to visit, but I just need some time alone with you for a while to recover from all of this." She looked down and added softly, "I don't want him to see me like this."

"Sweetheart, there are a couple of FBI agents outside the room. They're insisting on speaking with you. I made them promise to limit it to only a few questions. Are you up to it?"

"Okay," she said, placing the photo on the nightstand.

Rye poked his head outside the room and said, "You can come in, but just for a few minutes. My wife needs to rest."

The agents stepped into the room. "Mr. Field, we'd like to speak with her alone."

"I want my husband here," Dee replied.

"Mrs. Field . . ."

"You heard what she said. I'm not leaving her," Rye said, stepping beside the bed, taking Dee's hand, and sitting down.

"Mrs. Field, can you tell us what happened, beginning with when you first encountered your abductors?"

"My husband and I were at an awards ceremony. I was tired, so the driver took me home early. I insisted that Rye stay and enjoy himself. When I got to the house, I noticed the alarm wasn't on, but I thought maybe we just forgot to set it. I walked into the kitchen, saw them, and screamed."

"Had you ever seen them before?" the agent asked.

"Lucy looked familiar, but I couldn't place her. Then the man, Derrek, said her name and I realized who she was. He was holding a bag, which I later learned was filled with money they had stolen from our safe."

"Then what?" the agent asked.

"Derrek started yelling at Lucy, angry that she had said no one would be home. She said, 'Let's just take the stuff and leave,' and he said, 'She's seen us, we can't leave her.' Then it was as if a lightbulb switched on in his mind. He said, 'We could ransom her for a lot more than what we got here,' and he held up the bag. They argued for a couple of minutes and he pulled out a gun, pointed it at me, and said, 'We're taking her.'" She started to tear up. Rye squeezed her hand and rubbed her arm.

"I know this is difficult, ma'am. Please tell us what happened next," the agent said.

"I told them I was pregnant and begged them to take whatever they wanted and leave me, but Derrek was insistent. They forced me to go with them at gunpoint. On the way out the door, I discreetly turned over a photograph. It was the only sign I could leave my husband. Then we walked to their car, which was parked blocks away. Lucy knew how to avoid all the cameras. I pulled one of the rosettes off my gown and dropped it on the ground, hoping it would help you find me. They took me to the house and Derrek tied me to the chair. I kept begging them to let me go, so eventually he made Lucy put tape over my mouth," she continued, her voice cracking as tears slid down her cheeks.

"I think that's enough," Rye said.

"Please, we're almost done," the agent said. "Mrs. Field, what happened at the house?"

"They spent most of the night arguing about what to do with me. Derrek came up with a ransom plan and Lucy went along with it, but it seemed like she didn't want to, like she was afraid of him. He convinced her that my husband owed her the money. At some point, I nodded off. In the morning, Derrek started talking about how they couldn't let me go because I knew who they were. He was spiraling, and Lucy panicked. He set the gun on the coffee table, which is when Lucy sent him to the shed to get some more rope to make sure I was restrained. I didn't see what happened, but she came back alone. She told me that she had knocked him out and locked him in the shed, and not to worry, that no one would hurt me. Then she called Rye and we just waited for him to come."

"Mrs. Field, did they hurt you? You were there all night. Did anyone assault you?" the agent asked.

Rye took a deep breath as he waited to hear the answer.

"No," she said. "Just what I've already told you. I want to be helpful, but I'm so tired."

Rye stood up. "She's told you what happened. My wife needs to rest."

"Thank you, ma'am," the agent said. "We had everyone working on this. We're all glad you're alright."

"Thank you," she replied.

When they left the room, Rye turned and looked at her, unspeakable sadness in his eyes.

"Honey, please come here," she said, scooching over.

He took his shoes off and climbed into bed next to her. He put his arms around her and caressed the side of her face. "I love you so much," he whispered, pressing his mouth to hers.

"I love you too."

He rested his forehead on hers and said, "I'm so sorry, Dee. I'm so sorry."

"Honey, you didn't do anything to be sorry for. None of this was your fault. I knew you'd find me."

"I've never been so scared in all my life. If anything would have happened to you . . ." He broke down in tears, overcome by the emotion of the day.

"Do you know what the worst part was?" she asked, wiping away his tears.

He sniffled. "What?"

"I knew it would remind you of what happened to your mother, and how much pain that would cause you. That was unbearable. I would have done anything to take that away."

"You must have been terrified. I can't believe you were thinking about how I would feel while you were being *kidnapped*."

"I love you."

"Dee, I love you with all my heart. All my heart," he said, tucking her hair behind her ear, tears in his eyes. "You and our babies mean everything to me. All I want to do is take care of you."

"Kiss me, Rye."

He kissed her softly.

"I'm so tired," she muttered.

"I know, sweetheart. You go to sleep. I promise I'll be right here holding you."

She shut her eyes and fell asleep, safe in his warm embrace.

22

RYE WAS SITTING ON THE END OF THEIR BED WITH THE television on when Dee emerged from the bathroom, towel-drying her hair.

"It's true what they say, there's no place like home. It feels so good to be here with you, fed and clean," she said, walking over and sitting beside him.

He picked up her hand and kissed it gently. "It was hard to have you out of my sight even while you were showering," he said, tearing up. He gingerly ran his fingers across her bruised wrist, tracing the lines left by her restraints. "I can't believe this happened to you. I would do anything to take it away."

She rested her head on his shoulder. "This must be so awful for you. I know you felt helpless, but you saved me."

"Don't worry about me. I just want to take care of you."

"Rye, you've been through something traumatic too. This happened to both of us. I'm so sorry, honey. I'm home, safe with you now. The babies and I are home."

"You're wearing my old Metallica T-shirt," he noted, smiling sentimentally.

"It reminds me of our first night together."

He kissed her and said, "I fell completely in love with you that night. Being with you felt like being home."

She smiled. Their attention turned as they heard a report about

Dee's kidnapping on the evening news. "Oh my God," she mumbled. "The whole world knows."

"I can turn it off," Rye said, picking up the remote control.

"Leave it," she said. They showed Lucy and Derrek's mug shots, Lucy displaying the perfect angles of her face, a slight glint in her eye, a secret smile, as if she knew these would be the headshots finally seen around the world. This was her moment, and someday reality TV would come calling. Dee shuddered.

Rye rubbed her back. "No one will ever hurt you again."

Then they showed photographs of Rebecca Field, reminding the world how she had been slain during her marriage to Rye's father at the height of her fame. They brought in a panel of commentators to discuss parallels between the two events that forever changed Hollywood. "Tinseltown or Tinselterror?" the anchor asked.

Dee put her arms around Rye and whispered, "I'm so sorry. Turn it off."

He clicked off the television. "I'm going to have my management team release a statement and make it clear that we will never be speaking about this again. I'll keep the press away from you. I'll hire round-the-clock bodyguards to protect you and the babies."

"Honey, let's not worry about all of that right now. We need to find a way to heal and live a normal life. This was a horrible, freak incident. And the media, well, they'll lose interest eventually. They only have power if we give them our attention. We have much more important things to focus on," she said, rubbing her belly.

"I won't allow you to be subjected to this," he said.

"Rye, I've been thinking. Call the US attorney or have your lawyer do it. Try to persuade them to offer Lucy and Derrek some sort of plea bargain. I don't want to have to testify in court while I'm pregnant.

The stress of it," she said, shaking her head. "Please, the health of our babies has to come first. I don't want them at risk."

Rye took her face in his hand. "I'll take care of it. I promise."

"You look exhausted," she said.

"I can't remember ever being this tired in all my life," he replied. "Come on," he said, taking her hand and guiding her into bed. They lay pressed against each other. Dee rested her head on Rye's chest; he placed one hand on her belly and wrapped his other arm around her, and they quickly fell asleep.

The next day, Dee opened her eyes, still pressed firmly against Rye. Neither had moved an inch all night.

"Good morning, sweetheart," he whispered.

"Was it a nightmare? Did it really happen?" she asked.

He squeezed her and said, "It's okay, baby. You're home. We're together."

"What time is it?"

He craned his neck to look at the clock. "It's after noon. We passed out."

"I felt like I could sleep forever, like I was under a spell."

"Me too," he said.

"What about the show? You didn't go to work."

"They're shutting down production for a week so I can stay home with you. Longer if we need it. Nothing is more important to me than you and our babies. I won't leave you."

She held him tightly. He kissed the top of her head and told her, "I'm going to brush my teeth. Don't move; I'll be right back."

When he returned, she slipped out of bed and said, "My turn." They grazed each other's hands in passing. A moment later, Rye could hear muffled crying. He got up and stood outside the bathroom, leaning against the wall. When she emerged, she looked at him through her puffy eyes. He used his thumb to gently wipe away a tear she had missed. They stood for a moment in silence, staring at each other. She pulled her T-shirt off. He picked her up, she flung her legs around his waist, and he carried her to the bed. He pulled his clothes off and they began kissing passionately, exploring each other's bodies with their hands. "I love you with all my heart," Rye whispered, and they made love tenderly, their eyes glued to each other. After, they lay beside each other. He put his hand on her stomach and said, "Tell me what you need. Tell me what to do."

"You're already doing it."

The next morning, Rye woke up to find Dee sitting beside him, propped up against a stack of pillows.

"Hey. How long have you been up?" he asked.

"A while," she said softly. "I didn't want to wake you."

He stretched his arms and sat up. "Sweetheart, is everything okay? You look like you're a million miles away."

She glanced down and took a breath. "There's something I want to say to you, but I don't know how."

He swept his fingers across her hand. "You can tell me anything."

She looked into his eyes and said, "Maybe it's silly, but I never really saw you as a famous actor. I always just saw you as Rye."

"That's one of the things I love about you," he said.

"It's not that I was unaware that you're famous, but I always sort of looked at it as something unimportant or disconnected from who you really are, something to accept and not pay attention to. Kind of like if your spouse has an awful uncle who gets drunk at holiday parties and tells inappropriate jokes. That's just something you put up with once in a while because you love them."

He laughed. "I adore the way you look at things."

"Rye, something happened when I was with Lucy and Derrek, something I haven't told anyone about."

He snapped to attention, sitting straight up in bed. He placed his hand over hers and inhaled deeply. "Sweetheart, did they hurt you?"

"Oh God, no, nothing like that. I'm sorry. I didn't mean to worry you. It's just . . ."

"What?"

"I hadn't wanted to say anything, and truthfully I'm embarrassed to even bring it up, but I'm afraid it will fester if I don't."

"You can tell me. Please."

"After Lucy got off the phone with you, she was staring at me, and she kept looking at my wedding ring. She started saying things like, 'I don't understand how you got him. He could have been with the most beautiful women in the world. Why would he marry someone like you instead of someone like me?' And she went on and on about what a big star you are and how she couldn't grasp why you chose me."

"Sweetheart . . ."

"It's not like I'm horribly insecure. I've always felt fine about myself, and I know what we have . . . but I'm only human. I'm not a model or a movie star. She was right—you could be with anyone."

"I only want you. As for Lucy and her insane rantings, she's obviously unwell. If anything, she was jealous of you. Do you have any idea how mortified I am that I'd ever been with her in the first place?"

"I know, but . . ."

He put a finger to her lips. "Dee, you're the love of my life. From the first night we met, I just wanted to try to be worthy of you. Everyone who knows us knows that I'm the lucky one. I'm sure no one can figure out how I got you to marry me. I wake up each day in awe of you and feeling like I had better not screw things up because you're the best thing that could ever happen to me. You are beautiful, brilliant, talented, funny, and kind. You're the mother of my children. Sweetheart, no one else holds a candle to you."

"When we got married, I meant it forever." She placed her hands on her tummy and said, "I never would have done this with you if I didn't think . . ."

He cupped her face in his hands. "What we have is forever. You, me, and our babies."

She stared into his eyes and said, "I'm sorry. I feel ridiculous for having said anything."

"You have nothing to apologize for. I'm glad you told me. I'm so sorry for what you were subjected to, but it has nothing to do with us and what we have. She can't understand because she's never felt love like what we have together. This isn't something you need to ever think about again. I promise. I'm your Rye. You're my Dee. That's how it is."

"I know," she said quietly. "I've always known. I guess with everything that happened, I just needed to hear you say it."

He kissed her softly. "Baby, I'll say it as often as you want to hear it." He kissed her again, and they started running their hands along each other's bodies. They tumbled onto the bed and made love again. Rye whispered, "I love you," over and over again.

The days passed slowly as they stayed holed up in their home, nurturing each other and recovering from the trauma—snuggling and watching movies, listening to music, eating comfort food, and making love. Friends called and offered to stop by, but they chose to be alone together. Many sent flowers and food. Rose sent over homemade chicken soup, Lisette's recipe, which warmed Dee from the inside out. Lucy and Derrek each pled out and were sent to prison.

At the end of the week, they were sitting in bed. Rye serenaded Dee with his acoustic guitar, and when he finished playing, he set the guitar on the floor and said, "I'm going to call my agent and tell him they need to halt production on the show for a bit longer. Don't worry, I won't leave you."

"Honey, please don't do that. You should go back to work tomorrow. You're the star of the show. If you're not there, it affects the entire cast and crew. Go, make art."

He huffed. "Art? It's television. It's just entertainment."

"People need entertainment—the escape, the fun, the imagination. You're an artist who entertains people, beautifully I might add."

He smiled.

"Besides, I have to get back to my grant. The whole research team is counting on me. Plus, I have to prepare for that lecture at UCLA, which is less than two weeks away. If I get lonely, I'll call Troy to come keep me company."

He rubbed her faintly bruised wrist and said, "But sweetheart, you've been through so much. I don't feel right going back to work. I should be with you."

"Honey, it means so much to me that you want to take care of me. I love you more than I could possibly say," she replied, resting her hand on his strong chest. "When we decided to get married, we said we'd wake up and fall asleep in each other's arms each day, and then go out and do our own amazing things in the world. We can't stop because of this thing that happened. We can't forget who we are."

"Sweetheart, I don't know how to leave you. I'm, I'm . . ."

"What is it?"

"I'm afraid," he said, tears in his eyes. "If something happened to you or the babies and I wasn't there, I couldn't live with it."

She pulled his chin toward her and kissed him gently. "Rye, I love you so much. I know how awful this was for you, the way it stirred up memories of your mother's abduction and death. It tortures me to imagine how all of this made you feel."

"Sweetheart, you were held at gunpoint. The trauma of that doesn't just go away. I can see it in your eyes."

"It was terrifying, yes. Naturally, I still feel shaken up, but it will get easier. I'm okay. Our babies are okay. We need to be who we are. If we're not us anymore, what are we protecting?"

"Tell me you know that you come first to me."

"I do."

"If you need me, I'll be there, if anything happens with you or the babies, anything at all. Promise me you know that."

"I promise, honey. Look, it will probably be hard at first for both of us, but let's go out into the world and do the things we love. Remember that night when I taught Dazz's friend Chris how to concentrate and isolate things in his mind?"

"Circle, square," Rye replied with a faint smile.

"That's what we need to do to move on. Focus on one thing: your job. Besides, we really should work now. When the babies are born, I was hoping we'd both take time off to enjoy them."

"Of course we will," he said.

"Rye, I told you about that Sunday after I lost my mother, how my father was dressed and ready for our weekly breakfast. It was hard, and it was hard for a long time. I'm so grateful now that he taught me to go on with life, because it's precious and I don't want us to waste a minute of it."

He touched her hand. "He's a great father."

"And you will be too." She paused and said, "When my mother died, I turned to the arts—to escape, to find beauty, maybe even to find a purpose. You told me you did the same thing when you lost your mother. Let's do that now. I need to go advocate for art. You need to go make art. That's who we are. And then we'll remember that we're so lucky because we have passion for what we do in the world, and we have this incredible, passionate love."

He smiled. "An extraordinary life."

"Yeah," she whispered.

He pressed his mouth to hers, running his fingertips down the side of her face. "I love you with all my heart."

"I love you too."

23

THE NEXT MORNING, RYE'S ALARM RANG AT THE CRACK of dawn. Dee grumbled and rolled over. He kissed her head and slipped out of bed to get ready for work. Before leaving, he sat on the edge of the bed, stroking her hair. She opened her eyes and whispered, "Hey."

"I'm sorry I woke you, sweetheart."

"What is it, honey?"

"It's just hard to leave you." He paused. "I'll have my cell phone on me every second, even when we're filming. Promise you'll call me if you need anything."

"Promise," she said softly.

"There's a car and driver outside. The driver's name is Tom. He'll be here every day, whenever I'm not here, to take you wherever you want to go. There's also a bodyguard. His name is Theo. He'll be discreet, but he's there if you need anything or if you go anywhere."

"Rye . . ."

"Sweetheart, please. The media is still camped outside. Until the story dies down, I want you and the babies protected." He took her hand in his and gently caressed her palm. "It will make it easier for me."

"Okay," she agreed.

"Call me if you need anything at all. I love you," he said, leaning down and kissing her forehead.

"Love you too. Have a great day. Rye . . ."

"Yeah, baby?"

"Get lost in your work and have fun."

He smiled and said, "You too."

Paparazzi were waiting outside their home and at the studio, desperate to get a glimpse of Rye. They hollered, "How's your wife?" and "Do you think what happened to your wife is eerily like what happened to your mother?" He knew they were just trying to get a reaction. Rye ignored them, quickly hopping in and out of his car and whizzing past them. Once on the set, he called Dee three times throughout the day to check on her. He walked in the door at dusk and hollered, "Sweetheart, I'm home."

"In here," she called from the kitchen. "You're home early," she said, looking up from the papers she had strewn across the table.

"I missed you."

"That's sweet. I missed you too. I haven't even started dinner yet."

"How about I order some takeout?" he asked, leaning down to give her a peck.

She smiled. "Perfect."

"What do you feel like?"

"Anything, as long as there's no garlic. I'm reading the most fascinating article about art and emotional intelligence."

He smiled, just staring at her. She noticed and stood up. She ran her hands down his arms until they found his hands. "Was your day okay?"

He enveloped her in his arms, and she held him in return. "My day was fine." He sighed and said, "It will get easier."

Things did get easier as they both continued to work and go

about daily life. After a week with no comment from Rye or Dee, and thanks in part to a high-profile celebrity divorce, the media lost interest in the abduction story. A week later, Lou came to visit, which brought immeasurable joy and lightness to their home. After Lou returned to Florida, they focused on preparing the nursery for the twins. As his baby gift, Troy painted a whimsical mural on the walls depicting New York City at night and Los Angeles by day, a celebration of where the babies' parents came from. Susan took Dee out to lunch and shopping. As the mother of twins, Susan was a wealth of helpful information in the absence of the motherly advice that Dee and Rye both longed for. Every night, Dee and Rye snuggled in bed, content in the grace of simply holding each other. Once Dee could feel the babies moving around, from early fluttering to later kicking, Rye placed his hand on her tummy, smiling and laughing. He'd often pick up his guitar and serenade her and their unborn twins, playing the first song he wrote for her, and the others that followed.

24

RYE LAY BEHIND DEE, HIS NAKED BODY PRESSED TO HERS, his arm around her, his hand on her large belly. "That was so special. Thank you for making love with me," he whispered, kissing her between her shoulder blades.

"I'm just glad you still want me, thirty-seven weeks pregnant with twins. I'm enormous," she said, placing her hand on his.

"Sweetheart, I have never been more attracted to anyone in my life. You've never been more beautiful. Plus, we've had to get creative, which is fun."

She giggled. "Honey, I would love to lie here with you forever, but I have to go to the bathroom for the millionth time today."

He kissed the back of her neck and said, "I'll help you up." He got out of bed and slowly helped her rise.

She kissed him softly. "I'll be right back. Don't get dressed. I want to slip right back into your arms."

A couple of minutes later, Dee called from the bathroom, "Rye, you had better get dressed after all."

"Decided you've had enough of me?" he joked.

She opened the bathroom door and said, "Never. The babies decided they're ready to be born. My water just broke."

"Oh my God!" he said, jumping up and hustling into his underwear. "Don't worry about anything. The suitcase is by the front door. I'll call the hospital and let them know we're on the way." He was moving a hundred miles an hour, buzzing around like a busy bee.

"Rye," she said softly, urging him to slow down.

"Yeah, sweetheart?" he asked, walking over to her.

"Our babies are coming," she said, tears filling her eyes.

He smiled and gently touched the side of her face.

"How are you feeling?" the doctor asked.

"Tired but grateful for the epidural," Dee replied. "It's been nearly ten hours."

"You're doing great," the doctor said. "Let me just check and see how you've progressed. You're at eight centimeters and the babies are both in the head down position, just like we want. It won't be much longer now. I'll be back to check on you soon."

When she left the room, Rye put his cool hand on Dee's sweaty forehead. "You're doing great. I love you so much."

"Rye, I'm scared."

"Why, sweetheart? The doctor said everything is perfect."

"I know, but what if . . ."

"What is it, my love?' he asked, caressing her forehead.

"It's just that losing my mother was so awful, and if something happened to the babies or something happened to me . . ."

"Shh, nothing bad is going to happen. I promise you. I know it."

Just then, Rye's phone vibrated. He slipped it out of his pocket, checked the incoming text message, and said, "I have something that will cheer you up. I'll be right back."

"Please don't go."

"I promise, it'll just be one minute," he assured her, lifting her hand to his lips and kissing it gently.

He slipped out of the room and returned a moment later with her father.

"I heard a rumor that my little Deanna Banana is having her babies," Lou said with a huge grin.

"Oh, Daddy," she said, smiling brightly, her eyes lighting up.

Lou walked over, leaned down, and hugged her.

She looked at her father and then at Rye with an expression of confusion. "I don't understand how you got here so quickly."

"Seymour has had one of his jets sitting in Florida for weeks, waiting until we got word that you'd gone into labor. Rye sent a car service to pick me up at LAX. I asked him to keep it a surprise."

"It's the most wonderful surprise," she replied, tearing up. She looked at Rye, who was smiling, and said, "Thank you, honey."

"So, how are you doing?" Lou asked. "Rye said everything has been smooth sailing."

"Yeah," she said softly. "I just miss Mom so much. I wish she were here."

"Me too. She'd be so happy for you. You're going to be a wonderful mother."

"How long are you staying in LA? I want you to spend as much time with the babies as you can."

"Actually, that's my other big surprise. I don't want to miss a minute with my grandkids. Family is everything. So, about a month ago, I bought a place in LA."

"*What?*" she said, her eyes nearly popping out of her head.

Rye smiled so hard it morphed into laughter.

"I haven't even seen it. Found it online, fully furnished, and I asked Rye to check it out for me. He said it's only about fifteen minutes from you kids. I'll go back and forth between here and Florida.

Dolly said she's always felt like a California girl at heart, so she'll come with me, if that's okay with you."

"Of course it is. Nothing could make me happier." She looked at her father and then at Rye and said, "I can't believe you both did this."

"You're very loved," Lou replied, kissing his daughter's forehead.

"So are you," she said. "Both of you."

"One more big push, Dee," the doctor said.

"I can't do it," Dee moaned.

"Yes, you can," the doctor replied. "We're almost there."

"You're doing great, sweetheart," Rye said, wiping the sweat from her forehead. "You're so strong. I love you so much."

"Bear down and push," the doctor instructed.

Dee pushed with all her might.

"Here we go," the doctor said, ushering the first baby into the world. They heard their child cry for the first time. "You have a daughter," the doctor gleefully announced, handing the baby to a nurse.

Dee and Rye both started crying. The nurse helped Rye cut the umbilical cord and took the baby.

"I know you're exhausted, but I need you to push again. Your second child is ready. Push, Dee. Push, now."

Rye held her hand and Dee pushed with every ounce of energy she could muster.

"And here we are," the doctor said as the second baby entered the world and began crying. "Your second daughter is here!"

Rye cut the umbilical cord. He put his hand on Dee's face, both smiling and laughing through their tears. He leaned down and pressed his mouth lightly to hers.

"Are they okay?" he asked the doctor.

"They're perfect and they want to meet their mother," the doctor replied as she and the nurse put both babies on Dee's chest.

"Oh my God," Dee mumbled. "They're miraculous."

Rye sniffled and wiped his eyes. "This is the most beautiful sight I've ever seen, my three girls."

After a few minutes passed, the doctor said, "Let us clean them up a bit and wrap them in blankets." She and the nurse each took a baby.

Rye cradled Dee's face in his hands and whispered, "I love you with all my heart. All my heart."

"Rye, would you like to hold one of your daughters?" the nurse asked, handing him a beautiful baby girl. "Support her head and neck."

Rye looked down at his daughter and said, "I love you with all my heart too."

Dee smiled as the nurse handed her the other baby. "Would someone please get my father?" she asked.

"Certainly," the nurse said.

A moment later, Lou came bounding into the room. "Daddy, meet your two granddaughters, Louise Lisette and Riley Rebecca."

His eyes flooded. "They're amazing."

"Here," Rye said, handing him Louise. "Hold your namesake."

"She's so beautiful," Lou said, looking down at his tiny granddaughter.

"Does she remind you of Mom?" Dee asked.

"She reminds me of you."

Rye lay in the hospital bed beside Dee, stroking her forehead. "Thank you. Thank you for making me so happy," he said, kissing her softly.

"I love you so much," she said.

"I love you too, sweetheart, more than I could ever say."

The nurse wheeled the babies in, peacefully sleeping side by side. She handed one baby to Dee and the other to Rye. They lay together, staring adoringly at their daughters, a little family of four.

"Rye, do you remember the night we met when I said you can never hold on to magic?"

"I remember."

"I was wrong. Look. It's right in our hands. Gold dust."

Acknowledgments

THANK YOU TO THE ENTIRE TEAM AT SHE WRITES PRESS, especially Brooke Warner and Shannon Green. I'm incredibly grateful for your enthusiastic support. I also extend a spirited thank-you to Crystal Patriarche at BookSparks for helping readers find this book. Thank you to the early reviewers for your generous endorsements. Sincere appreciation to Shalen Lowell, world-class assistant and spiritual bodyguard. Heartfelt thanks to Celine Boyle for your invaluable feedback. Thank you to Clear Voice Editing for the always phenomenal copyediting services. Liza Talusan and the Saturday Writing Team—thank you for building such a supportive community and allowing me to be a part of it. The commentary about the arts throughout this novel was shaped by my decades as an arts-based researcher. I'm grateful to the countless scholars who have influenced the field and my thinking as reflected in this novel. To my social media community and colleagues, thank you boundlessly for your support. My deep gratitude to my friends, especially Vanessa Alssid, Melissa Anyiwo, Pamela DeSantis, Sandra Faulkner, Ally Field, Jessica Smartt Gullion, Laurel Richardson, Xan Nowakowski, Mr. Barry Shuman, Eve Spangler, and J. E. Sumerau. As always, my love to my family. Madeline Leavy-Rosen, you are my light. Mark Robins, you're the best spouse in the world. Thank you for all that words cannot capture. Bob Leavy, this novel is for you.

About the Author

photo credit: Mark Robins

Patricia leavy, phd, is a best-selling author. She has published over forty books, earning commercial and critical success in both nonfiction and fiction, and her work has been translated into numerous languages. Over the course of her career, she has also served as series creator and editor for ten book series, and she cofounded *Art/Research International: A Transdisciplinary Journal.* She has received over forty book awards. She has also received career awards from the New England Sociological Association, the American Creativity Association, the American Educational Research Association, the International Congress of Qualitative Inquiry, and the National Art Education Association. In 2016, Mogul, a global women's empowerment network, named her an "Influencer." In 2018, the National Women's Hall of Fame honored her, and SUNY New Paltz established the "Patricia Leavy Award for Art and Social Justice." Please visit www.patricialeavy.com for more information.

SELECTED TITLES FROM SHE WRITES PRESS

She Writes Press is an independent publishing company founded to serve women writers everywhere. Visit us at www.shewritespress.com.

Chuckerman Makes a Movie: A Novel by Francie Arenson Dickman. $16.95, 978-1-63152-485-1. New York City bachelor David Melman is a successful brander of celebrity fragrances. Laurel Sorenson, a leggy blonde, is a screenwriter on the brink of Hollywood success. When David, pushed by his bossy sister, agrees to take a screenwriting class taught by Laurel, an unlikely romance blooms—and that's just beginning of their troubles.

In the Heart of Texas by Ginger McKnight-Chavers. $16.95, 978-1-63152-159-1. After spicy, forty-something soap star Jo Randolph manages in twenty-four hours to burn all her bridges in Hollywood, along with her director/boyfriend's beach house, she spends a crazy summer back in her West Texas hometown—and it makes her question whether her life in the limelight is worth reclaiming.

Brunch and Other Obligations by Suzanne Nugent. $16.95, 978-1-63152-854-5. The only thing reclusive bookworm Nora, high-powered attorney Christina, and supermom-in-training Leanne ever had in common was their best friend, Molly. When Molly dies, she leaves mysterious gifts and cryptic notes for each of her grieving best friends, along with one final request: that these three mismatched frenemies have brunch together every month for a year.

Keep Her by Leora Krygier. $16.95, 978-1-63152-143-0. When a water main bursts in rain-starved Los Angeles, seventeen-year-old artist Maddie and filmmaker Aiden's worlds collide in a whirlpool of love and loss. Is it meant to be?